The Sharpener

and other stories

THE SHARPENER

and other stories

by

ANDRÉS BERGER-KISS

LATIN AMERICAN LITERARY REVIEW PRESS
Series: Discoveries
Pittsburgh, Pennsylvania
2005

The Latin American Literary Review Press publishes Latin American
creative writing under the series title *Discoveries*,
and critical works under the series title *Explorations*.

No part of this book may be reproduced by any means including
information storage and retrieval or photocopying except for short excerpts
quoted in critical articles, without the written permission of the publisher.

Acknowledgements
This project is supported in part by a grant from
the Commonwealth of Pennsylvania
Council on the Arts.

PENNSYLVANIA
COUNCIL
ON THE
ARTS

The title story, "The Sharpener," has been featured in the bi-annual anthology of Best International Short Stories, Europa Editions, Budapest, Hungary; the Instituto Nacional de Bellas Artes de México, México, D.F.; *Revista Chicano Riqueña: An Anniversary Anthology*, University of Houston, Texas; *Cuentos Hispánicos de los Estados Unidos*, Arte Público Press; "The Beggars," Chiricú Magazine, Indiana University.

Cover graphics by Heraclio Ramírez

© Copyright 2005 by Latin American Literary Review Press
and Andrés Berger-Kiss

Library of Congress Catalog-in-Publication Data

Andrés Berger-Kiss
   The sharpener and Other Stories / by Andrés Berger-Kiss
   p. cm.— (Discoveries)
   ISBN 1-891270-21-4 (pbk.: alk. paper)

PQ7298.12.E64A4513 2005
863'.64—dc22

2005017883

To Samuel Barchas and Cecile Pasarow-Barchas—who searched for the first editions of antiquity's masterpieces that comprise The Barchas Collection at the Stanford University Library—for encouraging my literary efforts throughout the years. To their librarian daughter, Sarah Barchas. And to Susan Adele Pasarow, light of my world.

A. B-K.

Contents

THE EMIGRANTS
Memoirs — Page

The Transylvanian deck of pumpkins and kings 13
The village of Gacsály 15
A long voyage 19
The girl who flew in a balloon 28
The sharpener 33
The poker players 41
The stamp collectors 59
The price of freedom 64
Two loves II 68
The night I met Lincoln 76
Cousins 77
In search of the past 79
"We're also human beings" 81

TROPICAL BLOOMS
Saint Weepy 89
Mario's Hideaway 97

PRE-REVOLUTIONARY SCENES IN LATIN AMERICA
The birth 101
The conquest 102
The duel 107
The recruit 114
The beggars 121
The priest 127

A FEW CHARACTERS IN THE VILLAGE OF SANTA BÁRBARA
The serenaders 139
The two fools of Santa Bárbara 142
The force of life 154

THE EMIGRANTS

The Transylvanian deck of pumpkins and kings

"I place my queen over your pumpkin," challenged one of the peasants with a flash of mischief in his eyes. He dropped a card on the little metallic table by the side of the fountain in the center of the village where he was playing with his three friends.

"I see you," said another peasant. "And I'll put my horse against your queen."

"So that's how you want to play," said the third one, taking out of a pouch a bit of tobacco which he jammed into his curved pipe. He saw the policeman, whose presence they had sensed and who continued looking at them from the nearby corner. Mumbling, one peasant warned the others: "Watch out! The man has not moved yet." He laughed and added in a loud voice to confuse the policeman. "I've got the best hand, the thirteenth of kings! Neither the pumpkin, nor your heart, not even the queen, much less the horse, can beat my hand. The king is always the winner. Long live the king!"

The fourth peasant, with a faint smile on his lips, half turned his head, his chin stretched toward his contender, fixed his glance on the edge of the sidewalk, to know the exact position of the policeman who had turned his back on the players, feigning interest in something else. Seeing the boots of the uniformed man and encouraged by a sly wink from the one with the king card in his hand, the peasant agreed with an exaggerated seriousness and exclaimed: "Yes, long live the king! With the king I'd get twenty points and you'd stay in the cellar with your pumpkin." He laughed and slapped himself hard on his thigh.

This Transylvanian deck of cards was found nowhere else in the world, unless a more rudimentary form managed to survive in Asia Minor from where it was taken by one of the first nomadic tribes of invading Magyars that established itself in Central Europe over a thousand years ago. The Gypsies used the deck to predict the harvests and to render their services as counselors in matters of love, health and money - what they considered the three most important possessions in life. The figures of hearts, pumpkins, horses, kings, sausages and queens now paraded in the multicolored deck, embellished with minute drawings.

The policeman continued his vigil in silence. Sometimes he lowered his head to sneak a look, fearing the peasants were plotting something nefarious. Few illegal activities ever occurred in the village but the policeman still received threats of demotion from his superiors should any act of insurrection occur during his watch.

The kings reigned in absentia for over a century from their unassailable castles in the outskirts of Vienna. Here, in the slopes of the Carpathian mountains of the old Hungary, in the province of Transylvania, everything seemed to be calm. The village, policed by a small garrison, was the most remote outpost of the empire, almost forgotten by the foreign power. But to the garrison in the center of the village, one block away from the square where the peasants sat playing cards by the fountain, dreaming of the day of their liberation, the instructions arrived from Vienna to maintain order and discipline, to insure there would never be an uprising. Armed policemen from the garrison plastered the edicts printed on posters all over the walls in the village. The peasants quietly stood before the announcements to learn the new weekly orders. They walked in groups of less than five. Any gathering over four persons was considered a punishable act of rebellion. Lesser infringements of the rules were fined. Jail sentences and sometimes beatings were imposed. In spite of the prevailing calm, an air of uncertainty, like the omen of a storm about to be unleashed, haunted the village.

The policeman made a wide circle around the players. It seemed to him that something strange was happening. He was certain the peasants were making fun of him and of his empire, even though, looking at them, he only saw these innocent looking ruddy faces with their handlebar mustaches, whom he knew lived off the earth, toiling in mud, eating dinner while they fed their animals. They are ignorant rabble who must be dominated, the uniformed man thought. Perhaps he should search them. But he had done so before and had come up with only a bunch of dirty handkerchiefs and a few coins. Nothing for which he could detain them. Why did they grin from ear to ear with their insolent smiles? He watched them for another hour, listening to their commentaries. At last, he shrugged his shoulders and slowly moved to the other side of the park. He turned around to look at them from afar through sheer habit. They were raising their hands higher than before, and were more animated as they slammed their cards against the table. These peasants are a bunch of slaves, he thought. As long as they have their daily bread they'll never rebel.

Now that the gendarme wasn't watching them closely, and remained too far away to hear what they said, the four peasants felt free. The one who had won the previous hand was shuffling the cards and as he dealt them, the cards were quickly picked up by the others. If the policeman had been able to hear what they were saying he would have dragged them to jail; he would have denounced them to the judge as traitors of the Empire; he would have beaten them during interminable nights in the dark cells of the garrison. For ten long years the peasants would have been forced to march each new day out of the filthy cells and made to work hard at the stone pits for having plotted against the kingdom.

But the peasants were out of hearing by the policeman, and instead of saying "pumpkin," they said "ass" or "face"; "king" was always followed or preceded by the word "tyrant"; the "queen" was "the whore"; the sausage was called "nose" or "penis. And the values assigned to the various cards were different. The king was worth less than a pumpkin. The social system had been turned upside down. Only the peasants understood what lurked behind their rules of the Transylvanian game of cards: The days of the occupation were numbered!

The village of Gacsály

In the last days of the Nineteenth century, the village of Gacsály was no more than a row of mud houses spread out on the arid steppes of the Eastern Hungarian plain. The Rosenfelds were living on the large estate where Jakab took care of the horses. Years later, when the Romanian armies gained possession of most of the country, there was a question as to whether Gacsály would remain in Hungary or in Romania. And much later, after men's folly had plunged the world into a second world war, the village almost became a part of what was then the Soviet Union. On both occasions, when the new frontier lines were drawn, the little village remained in Hungary, with both Romania and Ukraine only a few kilometers away.

Like so many of the villages in Eastern Europe, Gacsály remained nearly the same through the years. Once in a great while a new house was built at the end of the dirt streets and the village gained a few meters from the wilderness.

David ben Jakab had come to the village in the 1820's and after seventy years of managing the stable, settled down on the porch of his house, regaling generations of his offspring with the stories of his youth that he had kept to himself all his life. No one knew for certain how old he was, but his wife Sarah who, besides cooking and mending clothes, spent each day—except Sabbaths and holy days— embroidering the most lavishly colorful mantle pieces and bedspreads of the region, could prove he was over one hundred and twenty-five years old when he was finally put to rest. "He's always been thirty-two years older than I," she used to say. "So I know how old he is. I was born in 1810 and he in 1778." For the last thirty years of his life, until a few years beyond the 1000th anniversary of the birth of the nation in 1896—his life having touched parts of three centuries—, he sat on his rocking chair dressed in his colorful vest and plumed hat, with a large shepherd's staff in his hand and a pair of boots that came up snug to his knees, looking so much like a Hungarian peasant that no one suspected he had built a *mizrah* in the southeast corner of his bedroom where he prayed each morning and evening facing Jerusalem. Smoking his long curved pipe, wearing a handlebar mustache, David ben Jakab sat the children—one generation after another—on his lap while he unraveled his stories, many about their ancestors, sometimes going back into the recesses of the Middle Ages.

For the first ninety years of his life David ben Jakab had absorbed his experiences, saying only what was necessary, listening carefully and apparently hearing things no one else could hear, a trait that helped him predict pogroms and save his family on several occasions during his youth. When he finally sat down on his porch to listen to the shepherd's flute beckoning the sheep to return home and the barking of dogs herding them on the blazing horizon, he had nothing else to do but pour out the recollections of events no one else was old enough to remember. He loosened his tongue and did not stop talking. They said David ben Jakab, died with a twinkle in his eyes while he told his favorite story of the time he was traded for a horse. His grandson Jakab used to vie most successfully for his lap in order to hear the stories and when, in turn, he became an old man, repeated his grandfather's narratives to his son Imre's first child, who was always eager to sit in Jakab's lap and listen to the same old tales.

The story of the horse trade as told by David ben Jakab, imitated and revised by Jakab Rosenfeld as he narrated it to his grandson, David Rosenfeld, many years later in a big city far from the village, went something like this:

"Now come and sit here in your grandfather's lap my child, God's blessing be upon you, and listen to the old story of how your great, great, great, very great-grandpapa David ben Jakab—yes, the one whose name you bear—may it be written in the book of life, was traded for a horse a long, long time ago. I can tell you don't believe such a trade could ever happen! I can tell because your big blue eyes and your little mouth are wide open and you must be thinking: 'Dear Grandpapa, most wonderful of all Grandpapas—yes, I can almost hear you say those very words—, just what kind of a horse could this have been? Have you ever seen a horse? You have? Well, you never saw a horse like that, I can tell. For the horse great-great-grandpapa was traded for was no ordinary horse. He was not a work horse you see out in the fields plowing the hard ground. No! I can see you shaking your head *no* and you're right my blessed child. Was he then a horse to pull a wagon? Let's both shake our heads, no, no, nu, nu, nu! Was he a horse to pull a golden carriage? Not so, not so, not so! Was he then a horse, you might ask, for a great captain to ride to war, or for a king to prance around his castle? We must *both* shake our heads *no* even harder, for wars are the stupid ways of foolish men, and kings are the vainest among fools.

"Can you guess what was the color of the mighty white horse that was traded for great-great-grandpapa David ben Jakab? May they both rest in peace after all these years. Well? Can't you speak? Didn't I tell you it was a big white horse? His color was white! It was the biggest and friskiest horse, with the wildest eyes and strongest body that was ever seen in the whole world of those old days. When the owner of the farm where great-grandpapa had worked for many years saw that horse at the fair, he fell in love with it and spoke to the owner, who was a horse trader and farmer from a distant village of Gacsály. The man wouldn't take any money for the horse, saying that no one should ever ride on such a beautiful beast. But when he saw great-grandpapa David and found how strong and quick he was handling horses, and how even the wildest among them ate in peace out of his strong hands, they struck a bargain, a clean trade: a horse for a man's work. That is how our grandpapa David moved from the town of Kismarton to the small village of Gacsály and took his family with him, your very own granduncles and cousins who still live there."

Shortly after David ben Jakab's death, his wife Sarah tidied up the house, put on her best garments and, after embracing everyone, closed the door behind her and lay on the bed she had shared with him for over seventy years. Everyone knew she would never come out of that room alive. They summoned the rabbi from the community of Csenger—in winter a day's journey from Gacsály. Sarah had made practically no demands in her life and lived as inconspicuously as a shadow by her husband's side, always willing to do her chores without complaint. Now, in the hour of her death, she was as accommodating as ever. When the rabbi knocked at her door she quietly finished her recitation of the prayer before death—

the *Vidduy*—and, knowing who it was, she said in a faint voice, "God bless you, rabbi, please come in, I'm ready." By the time he opened the door and stepped through the threshold, she was dead, her eyes closed, hands neatly folded over her chest, looking as prim as ever, not a strand of hair out of place. All her embroidery projects were finished, ironed and meticulously stacked one on top of the other, forming colorful pyramids. To everyone's amazement, for it was not in her nature to ever make pronouncements, she left a handwritten note on the pile of ornamental needlework with only two words that apparently encompassed the philosophy of her whole existence and which no one in the family ever forgot. The note simply stated in small print: "Work redeems!"

It was her great-great-granddaughter Gizi, the oldest of Jakab's children, who discovered the note, read it out loud so all could hear and then kept it in her purse for the rest of her life. Of all her siblings, only Gizi worked as hard as Sarah, without expecting anything in return. It was Gizi who lightened her mother's work and who helped the elders even when she wasn't asked. Now that the pillars of the family were dead, Jakab and his wife Ida began to feel the weight of the years. The heavy work of caring for horses and farming someone else's property could never lift the family out of poverty. The notion of searching for their destiny elsewhere became prominent during the long talks they had in the evenings and on the Sabbath. Still, it was difficult to leave the security of Gacsály and venture into the unknown after so many years spent in the peaceful village. There was a sense of comfort there, especially when Jakab's two brothers, Mózes and Jenö, and sister Vilma got together with them.

On a cold December morning, on the first day of the celebration of the lights of Hanukah, Gizi walked out of her house to the main street of the village named after the poet Petöfi Sándor, and made her way toward the small Jewish cemetery where her great-grand-parents, David ben Jakab and his wife Sarah, as well as her grandparents, whom she had never met because they had died in the Revolutionary War—ending the brutal occupation of the foreign kings—lay buried side by side. Gizi, most devout of all the children in the family, often went to pray and talk to her buried relatives. As she approached the cemetery, she observed, even from a distance, the mounds of rubbish strewn across the main road onto the green bushes that encircled the cemetery. And when she entered she saw the obscenities written on the tombstones.

Gizi was not one to cry. She began to pick up the refuse and scrub the tombstones until they were clean again. She completed her work by noon and when she was through, she picked up a few pebbles and placed them on the graves. Bowing to her ancestors, she repeated the words of the *kaddish*, the mourner's prayer. But as she did, images of a pogrom began to interfere with her meditation. As she was finishing her prayer, the thought she had tried to disregard was formulated in such a clear way that by the time she said "Amen," she was sure she had been appointed to save the family from the next persecution, chosen to lead her loved ones to safety, to take on David ben Jakab's destiny and fulfill the family's belief that one of them would always be selected by God to save the rest. Gizi stood by the graves and said in a hushed, secretive voice, "Now I know that Gacsály is no longer safe for us. It will be dangerous here in our village and we must leave or we'll be surely killed. I will take you away in my heart where you will dwell until I die, until my own unborn children and their descendants will carry you safely in theirs." When Gizi left the cemetery she raised her voice: "Come with me now, let's find a safe place where you can all rest in peace." She walked feeling the full responsibility of carrying the souls of all the Jews buried there.

A long voyage

Shortly after departing the dock in Amsterdam, Lenke began to notice the up and down motion of the ship and was overcome by seasickness.

"Everything smells like fish," she said.

For the rest of her life, she abstained from eating any food that had grown in the sea. And if, perchance, a piece of fish was ever placed before her, she invariably sniffed it, shuddered and pushed the dish away much to the chagrin of her hosts. It didn't have to be a fish from the sea; any fish from a lake, a river or a pond suffered equal disdain and complete rejection.

Those first days of the voyage across the ocean were repugnant for David, unlike anything else he had experienced. Cooped up in the belly of the ship in a cramped cabin, with only a small porthole to look out to a cloudy sky with its incessant rain and the endless extension of heaving waters, the youngster missed his friends in the old neighborhood of Westeinde Street, the freedom in Den Hague, where he and his mother had waited for nearly two years to emigrate to South America.

Through the roaring of the storm, David endured Lenke's litany of personal distresses so keenly felt by her since her childhood, now intermittently regurgitated with the scarce food she took. The only surcease he experienced from this onslaught was sticking his head out the porthole, letting the drizzle refresh him, hoping to get away from her. But even then, he could hear his mother's complaints:

"Oh, I can't stand the constant roll in this stuffy place and its worse if I walk around. I can't keep any of this bad food down. It reminds me of the slop they gave me for years at the convent. Have I told you about how the nuns used to bang my head against the blackboard for being a Protestant? Please help me, my sweet boy who behaves like my dear little old lord, taking such good care of his poor mother. Get me the doctor, please; oh, I'm going to die."

David was unable to hold out and succumbed to seasickness also. The ship's physician conducted his examination, brought them hot tea, and explained there was really nothing so wrong with them that a good walk on deck and fresh air would not cure, adding that many people reacted the same way the first few days at sea. But as soon as he was out of sight, Lenke called him a quack who had no compassion for a sick woman and renewed her complaints.

At dusk, David tried to help her fight a pervasive insomnia to no avail. He scratched her little finger relieving the burning itch that tormented her during stressful times, while he told her again about the colorful talking birds they would see and the huge butterflies that flew sideways. Finally, deep into the black, oceanic night, they fell asleep.

David couldn't realize that a constant rain, cold and devastating, had fallen on his mother's soul since her childhood, miring her in the self indulgence of her constant lamentations and that, regardless of his efforts, there were no palliatives to lessen her many heartbreaks.

At the beginning of the third week, when the ship moved into less agitated waters as it approached Curaçao, they awoke to the sound of bells and great festive commotion on board. Someone banged the door of their cabin and yelled, "Come out and look at the sea!"

As soon as he heard the urging, David grabbed Lenke by the arm and told her, "There's something wonderful going on; we should see what it is!"

"I can't walk with the ship moving up and down," she answered. "But the boat is not moving like that anymore, Mother." He glimpsed out the porthole and saw a brilliant and blue sky. "Look, the dark days are gone! It's sunny out!" But Lenke covered her head.

He scrambled on the bed trying to open the porthole, since Lenke had shut it, fearing the wind and rain would come in. He looked out to the spacious sea, green and calm as an everlasting lake and gasped in awe, hardly able to contain himself for joy as he desperately tried to turn the crankshaft to open the small porthole. This was The New World all the neighbors had told him about. "Look, Mother, look," he screamed as he was finally able to stick his head out to look at the broad spectacle before him.

All of a sudden he had an unencumbered view of a world much more fascinating and glorious than his imagination could conjure up. He strained as the immense body of water before him was crisscrossed by hundreds of agile dolphins, their fleshy bodies darting at great speed in and out of the sparkling water, keeping up with the ship, leaping in unbelievable silvery ellipses near the ship, churning the placid waters into white froth, tumbling with the exhilaration of life that burst freely upon a magnificent universe that seemed designed to serve as their private playing ground.

David screamed out, unable to restrain his tears, moved by the gift this new world offered him after so many days of imprisonment, "The fishes! The fishes! Look at the fishes!"

All morning the dolphins swam around the ship while the passengers cheered them on, including Lenke, who finally allowed the child to coax her outside.

Everyone on deck seemed to know about the young woman who had been sick in her cabin with her child since the beginning of the trip and welcomed them. Lenke introduced herself, establishing a quick bond with a few others who found the ordeal of the stormy seas equally unbearable. They learned about her being a Hungarian actress and enrolled her, much to her delight, in a skit they were rehearsing for presentation on the eve of the ship's arrival in Curaçao. Lenke participated with such enthusiasm, pretending to be her country's ambassador on the SS Barnenfeld, challenging everyone to eat as many hot peppers as she did, proving that *Magyars* were the undisputed champions. It was difficult to believe she had been as sick as she claimed to be.

Dozens of canoes paddled by naked black children, eager to greet the ship as it entered the bay at Willemstad, escorted the Barnenfeld while the floating Köninging Emma Bridge swung open to let her into the colorful harbor. Surrounding the ship, the children's voices were heard all afternoon as they yelled to the passengers, "Maaaaneee! Maaaaneee! Maaaaneee!" They'd jump from their canoes trying to catch in mid air the elusive coins tossed from above and dive in pursuit of those beyond their grasp. The children would emerge smiling, showing their perfectly aligned white teeth while displaying the coin they had just retrieved from the sea. They put their treasure in their mouths and from time to time, spit out the silver into their canoes.

The ship stopped at several islands, sometimes for only as long as it took a few passengers to board a waiting motor boat which ferried them and their luggage ashore while the ship was already on its way out to sea again. In each port there were hundreds of children in the water surrounding the ship, yelling "maaaneee!"—their shining, naked bodies gleaming under the bright sun while the sound of wild and rhythmical music was heard from the villages.

Long lines of black men, strong and dripping with sweat, carried overwhelming loads on their shoulders over wooden planks connecting the ship to the dock whenever it anchored to unload some cargo.

Under the burning sun the faded pastel houses lined the hillsides away from the sheltered harbors where the native's boats sailed with the most varied assortment of tropical fruits. On the shores, the markets were full of fish still stirring in containers, and vegetables were sold by black women crying out the merits of their merchandise in a language strange to the Europeans, a mixture of an African dialect and Spanish.

As they approached the coast of South America, the crew warned all passengers about the mainland natives not being as honest as those in the island colonies. Lenke heard that thieves sometimes managed to come on board and was frightened.

"What if they steal my child?" she inquired of the Captain.

"They don't take people," he answered. "They have enough people to feed at home."

The earth, almost at the same level as the sea, was only a subtle line in the distant blue of a horizon so immense that the new world where they were headed seemed to be limitless.

A motor boat came out from the lagoon-like estuary of the Magdalena River by a place called Bocas de Ceniza (Mouths of Ash) and transported them a few miles upstream over the sleepy waters to the docks near the town of Barranquilla, where a three-decked stern-wheeler looking like a glittering palatial hotel, crammed full of passengers, was to carry them into the heart of the continent.

Only the sweltering incandescence of the unrelenting sun clearly in command of the pale blue sky, seemed to move, piercing with a devastating pressure like a gigantic iron leveling the ground and steaming up the river, and eventually converging upon the natives to keep them in a constant state of inactivity and boredom. Everything was still in the vast stagnation. Only the endless extension of the marshes was visible, molding pools with spots of tall swamp grass and now and then a stunted tree with its dry branches emerging like a solitary dwarf in the watery savannah, providing almost enough shade for one or two sleepy inhabitants to find comfort unavailable elsewhere. Occasionally, a mud hovel with an oxidized tin roof by the side of the river promised greater solace.

A light tune with a swingy, graceful rhythm, much in contrast with the surrounding indolence, greeted the few occupants of the small motor boat when it arrived by the side of the stern-wheeler. As soon as Lenke heard the first strands of the music played by six musicians on the top deck she was happy, convinced it was a variation of the same song her father had composed on the occasion of her birth. "They're playing my song," she said. Once before, in Den Hague, when the Royal Dutch Band led a parade in honor of Queen Wilhelmina, Lenke had seized upon one of the musical themes and announced to her bewildered relatives it sounded like the song her father had made up on the spur of the moment at the dawn of the new century.

The ship was called El Pichincha, named after one of the great battles in the war of Colombia's independence. With three decks, it had four classes although they sold reserved tickets for only the first three. Those in fourth class, paying as they boarded the ship, traveled next to a puffing steam boiler in the middle of the lowest deck at the level of the river. Almost all of the people in fourth class were blacks in rags, crammed one against the other in the suffocating heat. Many rested on the deck's metal floor on straw mats, lulled into sleep by the constant turning of the ship's huge stern-wheel's blades as they dipped in and out of the river accompanied by the relentless vibration of the roaring fire from the steam boiler as it consumed vast quantities of wood from the nearby jungles. Others, more fortunate, slept on their own hammocks which covered the crowded deck at night when it was nearly impossible to walk in the dark without bumping into sleeping people, some of whom moaned quietly, shivering with the fevers of malaria. The stench and discomfort were overwhelming since a small section next to the wheel was reserved for cattle, pigs, sheep and smaller, crated animals that attracted swarms of mosquitos.

It was through this deck, among all the curious people shoving to get nearer, that Lenke and David made their way toward the winding staircase leading to their second class quarters, guided by the ship's officials who kept pushing the natives to make room.

"Why do they have their hands out?" David asked. "Do they want to touch us?"

"They want money," Lenke answered, frightened, clutching the child and covering her nose with a perfumed handkerchief. But later they found out the natives also wanted to touch them because many had never seen a white-skinned blonde.

As the boat began to move, both the smell and the mosquitos vanished, but they returned whenever the boat stopped at the many villages along the river. In the late afternoons, clouds of mosquitos invaded the boat.

"Between five and seven its best to lock yourselves in your cabins, if you don't want to be eaten alive," the Captain advised everyone.

After three days, the dryness of the surrounding forest slowly gave way to the gigantic green entanglement of a dense and humid jungle. The river became a maze of shallow lagoons whose waters were nearly still, where the main channel changed with the seasons. They came to a halt when the Magdalena River ran out of water. Mired in the muddy bottom, the jungle almost at arms' length, they waited, the trapped sternwheeler slightly tilted, its immobility encouraging the hungry alligators to come closer during the night.

"We'll have to wait until it rains further inside the continent, up in the mountains," the Captain informed the passengers. Impeccably dressed in white, his starched lapel flashing a large silver medal which he kept polishing automatically with his sleeves, the captain insisted on being in charge of every maneuver each time the ship came to port or weighed anchor. "According to my calculations it rained yesterday and we should be getting the fresh water in two days," he added, squinting his eyes as he looked into the blazing sun.

Lenke walked up to him while he made his daily inspection tour of the ship, indicating there was no air for her to breathe when the boat stopped. He slowly understood and laughed. "Air? Air?" he asked. "Air is all around us. All you have to do is breathe in. It's easy!" He demonstrated with great zest while those around him laughed and joked about the beautiful foreign lady who didn't think there was enough air in Colombia, one of them jesting, "Air is mainly what we have in this country! You came to the right place, *señora*."

The Captain invited Lenke to the uppermost deck, where only first class passengers were allowed. A slight breeze relieved her somewhat but what amazed her was the luxury in contrast with the rest of the ship: the cleanliness and abundance of food. She could not bear the thought of having to return to their cramped and sweltering little cabin and share her second class accommodations with passengers in third class who used the same dining room and slept outside the cabins on deck chairs and hammocks strung during the night. After she inquired about the difference in price, she took out a few of the English pound notes her father had given her and placed them in the purser's hands. He immediately ordered a servant to bring up their belongings.

"Now we can wait for the fresh water in peace," she told David. "I don't think the alligators can make it up this far." She shuddered.

During the week they were stranded in the middle of the jungle, David learned enough Spanish to begin asking questions. Although Lenke was afraid to let him mingle with the passengers below and for the first two days only allowed him to walk downstairs in the company of a steward, later David went everywhere by himself thanks to the Captain, who liked to expand on his private theory that the only virtues boys of any age lacked to be men were experience and a larger set of balls. He made fun of Lenke's worries and took her down to meet the natives, reassuring her there would be no danger for the boy on any vessel under his command, adding, to quell her hesitations, "The bad smell is only due to the animals and not the natives who bathe in the river whenever they are hot and are cleaner than any of us." She understood the man's gestures but not a single word he said.

David's favorite place was among the black people in fourth class. He learned to fish and also how to touch an alligator's tail when the animal was looking the other way. Of course, Lenke didn't see him and he never told her. But the creatures were so trusting, they came close to the boat and lay there, staring, for hours.

Each day while they waited for the river water to arrive, they were awakened at dawn. As the last stars blinking in the opalescent sky slowly faded into the grayish blue of the new day, a flock of screaming birds— parrakeets and parrots with most colorful feathers— darkened the sky and came to rest on the ship. David awoke before their arrival and watched them leave until they blended into the jungle's horizon, their screaming slowly fading in the great distance. Their clamoring was replaced by the wild gibbering of a multitude of monkeys jumping from branch to branch as if they were intent on outdoing themselves, performing unbelievable acrobatic stunts, some climbing between the stern-wheel's blades of the immobilized ship to reach the upper decks.

On the seventh day of their wait, the fresh waters began to swell the river, lifting the boat. "My calculations were correct," the Captain announced as he looked through his field glass at the oncoming clouds, "but it took more days for the water to get here because it ran down the other side of the mountains first, toward the Orient. Sometimes the Amazonian basin gets the first rain. But now it's our turn."

Lenke insisted that, while the boat was moving, David had to stay on the upper deck. The boy was sorry to see the rains come, to give up the sight of the early birds and the daily monkey invasion, the fishing and his wanderings around the boat, his new friends in the fourth class who taught him his first words in Spanish.

When the rains began, the natives stopped singing in the evenings and David missed hearing their chants accompanied by the sounds made with sticks and tin plates. And he thought about the clear nights when he and Lenke counted stars and sat for hours listening for the faint whispers of the jungle surrounding them, hearing the splashing of fish and the close and distant wailing of beasts hidden in the impenetrable shores, the wild and plaintive calls lingering on the horizon. The soaring sounds blended harmoniously with a glorious cadence into the magnificent symphony that was nature's own simple reaffirmation of life.

When the rains came, no other sound except the splash of water could be discerned, and a gray curtain, swept by the southern winds, covered everything. The ship was like a steam bath as the torrential waters poured steadily down.

"Now I know how Noah felt in his ark during the deluge," Lenke said, looking out the window, no longer able to see the shore.

The flood made it difficult for the ship to move up the river and as soon as the evenings came they'd anchor usually by a small settlement. A few days after the rains began, Lenke got up one morning and was puzzled viewing the village where they were moored. "Did they build these towns alike?" she inquired through gestures and the few words she learned and which she mixed with Hungarian. "This village looks exactly like the one I saw yesterday." Although she could not speak the new language, if she wanted to communicate anything, there was no way to hold her back.

"It is the same," the Captain answered, blinking. "The waters carried us downstream while you were asleep."

For three more days they waited in a town called Barrancabermeja while the turbulent river raged around them. On the fourth day the waters subsided and the usual calm returned, but many damages to the ship had to be repaired. When they arrived in Puerto Salgar, the last port of call, exactly three weeks had transpired on a river trip normally lasting eight days, almost as long as it took them to travel across the ocean.

In Puerto Salgar, an employee from the railroad came to meet Lenke and David with a letter from Imre, letting them know he had come down three times on the day-long trip from Bogotá only to find out their ship was still delayed, with no word as to when it would arrive. Two railroad tickets were enclosed with instructions. The short note ended by saying: "Since Bogotá is a place where nobody has any accurate information, I don't know when your boat will arrive but will be at the railroad station every evening to meet you. Love, your husband (& Papa.)"

Early next morning, when Lenke and David boarded the train, it seemed as if the whole town had gathered at the railroad station to sell its wares or beg. The ships of the Magdalena River came and went at all hours of the day or night, but the train's departure for Bogotá at six every morning was the only event in town everybody could count on. Departures were a happy occasion. The sleepy passengers were constantly besieged by peddlers. Most of the negotiations took place through the train's open windows where the travelers, once securely accommodated in their seats, leaned out to hunt for bargains, prices dropping precipitously as the time for departure approached. Some of the more enterprising salesmen remained on board to finish their transactions while the train picked up speed, and waited to get off in one of the steep bends of the cordillera where it slowed down to such a crawl that many of the adolescents got off the train jesting about how slow the train was as they pushed it.

The first time Lenke took a good look at the awesome abyss looming so close to the tracks that the train seemed to move over air, the itch in her finger returned. "I must remember to stay away from trains," she told David, who was interested in pursuing a friendship with another child.

High up on the Andean mountains not far from Bogotá, when the oppressive heat had given way to a fresh breeze and a subtle fog slid by the ravines, the train stopped at a village on the cordillera's edge to have the order of the cars rearranged. The passengers were told no one could be on the train until the cumbersome operation was completed.

Lenke and David sought the solace of the far end of the station to avoid the crowd.

Contrary to the curiosity they had aroused among the natives on the ship and along the river villages, the natives in the uplands of the interior seemed aloof, though from a distance they'd cast surreptitious glances at the white travelers, never coming close to the strangers. Many of the natives wore a profusion of hand carved jewelry. Men and women looked alike: their bodies covered by drab ponchos coming down to their knees, with their hair cut in a blunt square, low across their forehead, just above the eyes.

With his back turned toward the station, an Indian leaned out over the edge of a cliff, playing a flute which he held up toward the sky. The melody had a haunting sound, sustained and piercing, whose echoes reverberated through the precipitous canyons among the magnificent pinnacles, leaping out of the fog that spread over valleys of unsurpassed beauty as they revealed themselves from time to time in the great distances below.

"Does it remind you of the song Grandfather Bártfai composed for you?" David asked his mother, holding her hand, half teasing her.

"No," she answered to his surprise. "I have never heard music like this before."

They waited for a while, listening, overwhelmed as the song spread out over the immense vastness and majesty of the land surrounding them.

"It is the most sorrowful, plaintive sound I have ever heard," Lenke said. "These people must know what sadness is." But the boy loved the strength in the music, its yearning for freedom.

The girl who flew in a balloon

She was a little dark-skinned girl six years old and she had four tresses that hung to her waist. She was very poor and always ran barefoot over the pointy stones of the street where she lived, called Chumbimbo, named after the black seed of the weed that grew on the slopes of the mountain nearby. When we least expected, she decided to fly over the city of Medellín.

What happened, happened before the airplane, the rocket, the dirigible, the helicopter, or any other flying machine polluted the peaceful skies of Antioquia, a place full of mountains in Colombia, in the tropical part of the continent, when the only things that could fly in those old days were the big, multicolored Christmas balloons and the buzzards that made circles in the sky.

Each morning the little girl came out to the door of the hut where she lived with her aunt, Misiá Zoila, who had brought her and her three brothers from the village of Fatlies. While Misiá Zoila braided her four tresses, the girl looked astonished toward the Hill of the Sugar Loaf which emerged powerful above the huts at the end of the street of sharp stones.

The idea of flying from the Chumbimbo back to her village of Fatlies, taking first a peek through the high arches of the main tower of the Cathedral's belfry and a look around the Hill of the Sugar Loaf, among the clouds, entered into that little stubborn and clever head while she stared at the multicolored balloons which ascended by the hundreds toward the sky the first day of December. Her name was Marylita but she never lost the opportunity to recite her complete name.

"So your name is Marylita!" said a neighbor lady after she arrived from her village.

"Sí señora," she responded with the greatest courtesy. "But my true Christian name is…" —and here she paused to take a great breath of fresh air—"….Mercedes Ana Mary Peláez Carrasquilla Botero Montoya Suárez Moreno Díaz García Ramírez Restrepo Vásquez Zea Uribe Mejía."

Three or four times she filled her lungs with air without stopping the recitation of her surnames.

"Is Misiá Zoila your mother?" the neighborhood's storekeeper asked her once in my presence.

"No señor," answered Marylita, beginning to get ready, forcing air into her lungs. "She is my aunt and I am from the village of Fatlies and if you want to know, my name is…" —and she went on in order, until she said all her names. They used to say in the neighborhood that Marylita repeated her names at least four times a day and no one ever heard her make a mistake repeating them proudly and clearly so everyone would hear them.

I was seven-years-old then and was Marylita's boyfriend. And Juaco, who was the neighborhood drunkard, at all hours sitting on the ground at the end of the Chumbimbo street, usually holding on to a bottle of alcohol between his thighs, was our friend and confidant.

Juaco and I were the only ones to my knowledge who memorized Marylita's complete name. That is why she loved us so! It was very difficult for Juaco, who already had the white whiskers of an old man, to learn such a long string of names. Not only had the natural course of aging played havoc with his memory, but also the alcohol had damaged his brain in such a cruel way that he could hardly remember his own name and was always making terrible mistakes pronouncing even the most common words.

At the end of much practice after my school hours, Marylita's true name was imprinted in the remains of Juaco's memory, so that upon seeing her running toward him on the sharp stones of the Chumbimbo he exclaimed on a certain day as though it were the most usual thing in the world:

"Dare comes old Mercie And Maryjell Pilly Rascaltequilla Butter Toy…." He stuttered painfully, mixing up some of the names but trying for all of them and, losing the entire reserve of the air carried in his lungs, he took a long drink before finishing the list.

Marylita felt so loved by us and was so moved, sensing our uncommon effort, that she confided her secret to us:

"I am going to fly in a balloon from the Chumbimbo, around the Cathedral's belfry and up the Hill of the Sugar Loaf, clear over to my village of Fatlies!"

At first we didn't give much importance to this declaration, thinking it was one of her many passing fancies. But when one day Juaco, in one of his sober moments, and I went to the corner shop to purchase the eight sheets of paper it took to make one of the balloons that were daily elevated from all the neighborhoods of the city, Marylita blocked our way, saying:

"Make me a balloon for Christmas with more, more paper, so I can fly away in it. Huge, like this," she concluded, extending her arms as if to embrace the whole street. And then, not to miss her chance and gesturing like a grown up woman, she added proudly, "That's the wish of Mercedes Ana Mary Peláez…." —and she continued with all the rest of her names. When she started her recitation, there was no way to stop her. She was like a wound-up toy.

Juaco and I made her the biggest, most colorful and fanciest balloon that had ever been seen in Medellín. It was so big it could not fit in the little street. And Marylita was so happy watching its progress and helping us make it that she could hardly contain herself. It took us ten days to build it and we decided that Christmas eve would be the best day for her flight.

The week before the flight I became very ill. A typhoid epidemic swept the neighborhood and many of the poor of the Chumbimbo and some of the richer folks of the street next to it, where I lived, fell prey to the fevers. The only thing I remember of the many weeks I was almost unconscious in the hospital before I recovered, is that frequently I felt at the threshold of a terrible darkness which was like the very center of an immense tunnel without end. Each time that darkness began to engulf me and drag me to a place beyond my dreams, the pure and happy light from the colors of Marylita's balloon, ascending with her toward the sky where the sun promised new life, rescued me. I saw her smiling with her four tresses, way up high, waving good-bye with her dark little hand, and it made me feel better.

After a long convalescence my parents allowed me to go out to the street again. The first thing I did was to look for Juaco at his usual place.

There I found him drunker than ever. He hardly recognized me in his stupor. At least, that is what I thought because when I shook him he gave me a long look and covering his face, he refused to speak. When I insisted, asking him about Marylita and her balloon, he turned away from me.

"Leave me on," he said, not wanting to answer my questions. He meant to say, to leave him alone, but I was quite well accustomed to his manner, to understand his twisted words and the peculiar gyrations of his speech—after all, he was my best student. Then he suddenly smiled, as though a great idea had occurred to him and began to tell me about Marylita's flight.

She was placed in a special box under the balloon. Her four tresses had ribbons: two yellow, one blue in the middle and one red, which were the colors of her country's flag. All the people from the neighborhood came to see her fly on Christmas Eve. Juaco went on to tell me that the last words she had said after reciting her full name was a message—to forgive her for flying away without saying good-bye to me. She went straight up and followed a cloud to the Cathedral's belfry before heading toward the Hill of the Sugar Loaf.

I had never heard Juaco speak for such a long time. His words were so well tied together that he even surprised himself. But suddenly he avoided my eyes, closing his humid eyes and began to suck the bottle until he emptied it completely. It finally slipped out of his hands and bounced on the sidewalk out of his reach, breaking in the gutter. He was out and I knew there would be no way to wake him up the rest of that day.

When I went to the storekeeper at the corner to ask for more lucid details, he busied himself with his chores and curtly said he didn't have time to talk. I insisted and at last he stopped and looked at me with a strangeness in his eyes, not knowing what to say. Finally he came out to the door of the shop and showed me the exact course of Marylita's flight around the city.

"You see the sky?" he asked me, pointing with his finger. "She went straight to the Cathedral...in that balloon, stopping in mid-air in front of the belfry while the bells were tolling just as she had planned it. All the people saw her off, waving to her and saying good-bye to Marylita. And then she turned around and went up toward the Hill of the Sugar Loaf, on her way to the village of Fatlies where she will....live forever."

Suddenly, he became very serious as though he had regretted having talked to me and lowered his head thoughtfully. "Don't ask me any more questions," he added, "I have to attend to my work, boy." And he disappeared behind a black curtain in the back of the shop.

I went to see Misiá Zoila, Marylita's aunt, and she assured me that everything I had been told by the others was pure truth and added that the balloon had taken her clear into the village of Fatlies where she was in good health. I thought she missed Marylita very much because she could not stop crying while she spoke.

"Some day," she finished saying, "we will see her."

I returned often to talk to Misiá Zoila and hear her tell about Marylita's flight from the Chumbimbo to the village Fatlies, to find out how Marylita was and to receive the greeting she always sent me from her village, saying she was well and thinking of me. Misiá Zoila almost always cried talking about her, but was eager to see me even if it made her sad.

I never saw Marylita again.

The years passed and my family moved to a new neighborhood far away from the Chumbimbo. I got very busy growing up and almost never thought again about Marylita.

But now that I live ten thousand kilometers from the Chumbimbo I look from time to time at the same starry sky and I remember my first little girl-friend, the one who is most precious because she belongs with the dream of childhood, and a world from the very distant past revives then in my heart.

I knew that Marylita never flew in the super balloon. Drunk and disheveled, lost in the stupor of his alcoholism, Juaco was not a good liar. I knew the moment I asked him that Marylita had died in the typhoid epidemic. And when I asked the shopkeeper at the corner I confirmed my convictions. When I spoke for the first time with Misiá Zoila I was sure they had buried Marylita during my illness. I knew they didn't have the money to take her to a doctor and much less to a hospital.

I let all of them lie to me! And how I loved them for those lies! Juaco, for trying in the midst of his drunkenness to save me from the pain that knowing what happened would cause me, adorning as best he could in his terrible condition the fantastic tale he could hardly weave with the last traces of words within the reach of his deteriorating brain and which he used perhaps for the last time to defend a child's dream; the shopkeeper, for lying straight out in spite of his wish to teach me not to be afraid of the truth; and Misiá Zoila for keeping a hope alive, for maintaining with me a conspiracy of lies knowingly, pretending that the little girl we both loved still lived. I knew the truth from the first moment. No one deceived me and I suspect they also knew that I was aware of the truth, that we were all pretending she still lived.

Even now, after so many years, when I look at the starry sky so far away from the multicolored balloons of my childhood, I hope you no longer have to run barefoot on the sharp stones that hurt, that neither the typhoid not the other illnesses and terrors of poverty take you away or harm you, Mercedes Ana Mary Peláez... Carrasquilla... Botero... Montoya... Suárez...Moreno...Díaz... García... Ramírez... Restrepo...Vásquez...Zea...Uribe... Mejía... dear little dark one of the four tresses that hang to your waist: two with yellow ribbons, one blue and the other red.

The sharpener

The city of Medellín began to absorb immigrants scattered by the menace of the approaching European disgorgement just before World War II. Among them was a man who made a strong impact on the children of the town. He rode on a tricycle with huge wheels and a yellow parasol mounted on top of an enormous green box filled with tools used to sharpen knives and scissors. Every Saturday he came to the neighborhood where the Rosenfelds lived at exactly nine o'clock in the morning, announcing himself with a flute he played with one hand. As soon as the children heard that series of repeated dissonances ending with a note sustained for several seconds, they came out of their houses in droves not only from the recently paved Avenida Echeverry but also from the adjacent little street of El Chumbimbo, one of the poorest in the city.

The children would interrupt whatever they were doing to watch him work at the intersection of El Chumbimbo and the Avenida Echeverry where he usually parked his tricycle. He was known as "the sharpener" because the big box from which he took out all kinds of oils and instruments carried that announcement in thick red capital letters. When the sparks burst from the sharpening wheel, the children remained absolutely mute.

He wore glasses with only one very powerful lens that enlarged his blue and penetrating eye into a colossal and frightening size. Only the socket remained of his other eye. He said his eyeglasses had a permanent open window for ventilation but when the sparks flew through that opening, falling in the very depths of that empty purple socket, the children were petrified, transfixed in a hypnotic trance.

No matter how often he told how his eye was lost in a hand-to-hand combat with a Fascist soldier in the Spanish Civil War, the children remained convinced it was the sparks that burned a hole in his eye and blinded him, and that all the stuff about barricades and bayonets was only a tale.

In his first conversation with the children, the man became annoyed at the curriculum of the schools in Medellín because they did not teach the evolution of the species.

"It would be better if they'd teach you the theory of evolution," he told David, looking at him straight in the eyes. He proceeded with the first of many lessons he gave throughout the years: "Man, that is to say Homo sapiens, according to the discoveries of Carlitos Darwin, came from the monkey." He stopped sharpening for a few seconds and gazed with his penetrating eye at his audience. Ceremoniously reaching into his vest pocket he brought out a map of the world to trace the voyages of Charles Darwin to the Galápagos Islands. As he did, he assigned various roles to the children surrounding him, saying to Chucho, "You'll be the captain of the ship;" to Jacinto, "You'll be one of Carlitos's scientific assistants;" to José, "You man the dingy;" and to David, "Take notes on all the observations." To Fernando, who burst out in gleeful laughter and applauded every time the sharpener came to the neighborhood, he said, "You grab the rope that holds this expedition together." The sharpener reserved the role of Darwin for himself, ordering Captain Chucho to navigate toward the north where the sought-after specimens could be found and told Jacinto to get right into La Loca stream and fetch a turtle for his study, explaining all along the theory of evolution.

Peace reigned in Medellín even though the number of poor people turned mendicants seemed to be increasing out of proportion to the rest of the population. The only scuffles took place at soccer matches among inebriated fans, or between political rivals during elections when the town was sealed and no one could buy any alcoholic beverages.

Each Saturday, the sharpener came as usual and greeted the new additions to the neighborhood: "Russian boys, eh? And an Antioquian from the village of Santa Bárbara? And we have our Hungarian boy, of course. And I from the garden of Spain, Asturia! We have a lot to learn from each other!"

After he finished his work, he continued where he left off the previous week and brought out of his vest pocket a drawing of a creature with features resembling both man and gorilla.

"No matter what part of the world we come from, or whether we're black, white or yellow, this is the picture of our grandfather," he said to the children gathered around him. And in a nonchalant way, he added, "His name was the *Pithecanthropus erectus* and he lived millions of years ago. We all descend from him. All of us are nothing but a bunch of sons of monkeys!"

The children looked at the picture stupefied. The ferocious beast had a faint resemblance, inexplicable and bewildering, to Raúl, the bully who was the strongest boy in the block, a thirteen year old who was quite a nuisance, always getting into trouble. As soon as the children saw the picture, they began mocking Raúl behind his back, calling him Raulóntropus sonoffamonkus, but the sharpener defended him. Without exception, he always defended the weak and those who needed help against any form of injustice. "Don't make fun of Raúl," he explained. "He might become the president of the republic someday." Everyone looked at Raúl who was smiling and sucking on a huge mango and for a moment they saw him already grown, displaying the yellow, blue and red flag across his chest, as the Excelentísimo Presidente de la República de Colombia in a very serious pose without the mango stain that went from ear to ear. The sharpener always made the children think of the future.

That same afternoon, when Doña Rafaela, the mother of Raúl plus eight other children, asked him what the sharpener had said, the boy responded he was told his grandfather was a monkey and that all people—red, blue or any other color—are a bunch of sons of monkeys; that it was better to forget the tale of Adam and Eve because it was mere invention and that he might become the president of the republic and therefore he shouldn't be spanked anymore but treated with respect.

Hearing the account, she screamed to heaven, "I knew that man was a good-for-nothing atheist sent by the devil himself, teaching absurdities to my child!" She forbade Raúl to ever talk to him again. But during the sharpener's next visit, when he promised to teach the children how to hypnotize and obtain complete control over parents, Raúl didn't miss a word from his hiding place.

The sharpener taught the children to mistrust those who profit from the work of others. "The earth belongs to the peasants who work with it and the factories belong to the workers who toil there," he said, raising a fist. So the lesson would hit home, he taught Alberto Durango, the stingiest boy in the Avenida, to sharpen knives. Then he allowed him to sharpen four knives while he sat down to smoke a pipe by the shadow of one of the tropical trees everyone referred to as "pisser trees" because they produced an interesting bud which, when squeezed, squirted a long stream of yellow liquid. When Alberto was through, the sharpener charged the customer twenty cents and, giving only two to the boy, he pocketed ostentatiously the rest while he looked at the children without blinking that penetrating blue eye of his. Then he asked, "Does it seem fair to you that I should earn eighteen cents from Alberto's work smoking my pipe under a pisser tree while he earns only two working under the hot sun?"

One Saturday morning the sharpener played the part of Leonardo da Vinci and after showing the children a book with colorful photographs of paintings, he unraveled the great master's helicopter plans. He first ordered Abrahán and Vladimir, the recent arrivals from Siberia, to make a basket out of loose straw. Hernán—the boy from Santa Bárbara—was to signal the moment of departure. David, the Hungarian boy, was in charge of the blueprints. Little Chucho reported on the direction of the wind while Fernando held the rope again. After Doña Rafaela forbade Raúl from speaking to the sharpener, some of the mothers of the neighborhood, victims of the campaign she spread against him, began to feel uneasy, jealous because the children copied his manners and attitudes, often repeating what he said. But that apprehension was suddenly transformed into a profound dislike of the man upon hearing that his lessons had taken a turn toward what some of them called "the shiftless and prohibited themes."

On a Saturday when the boys, as usual, surrounded the sharpener, a new maid appeared who had just received employment at Hernán's home. Neither David nor Hernán, nor any of the boys of the neighborhood, had seen her before. She arrived from Santa Bárbara the previous night, innocent and provincial, never having seen a city. Now she walked, spirited and brisk, like a true native, directly toward the sharpener with a bagful of knives and scissors from Hernán's home. Her name was María Elena.

For almost an hour the sharpener worked in a silence interrupted only by the monotonous sound of the sharpening wheel. Never had such quiet reigned in the Avenida. The boys, with the exception of Augustico who was afraid of girls, stared at the newcomer while the sharpener's sparks had definitely lost their attraction. Hernán seemed a little taller and especially paler than usual, breathing deeply with his mouth open and swallowing saliva from time to time, without being able to take his eyes off María Elena's breasts.

David nudged him and whispered, "Have you ever seen anything like that?"

"Never, never," Hernán answered, mesmerized, swallowing again. "Not even in my dreams." As soon as her utensils were finished, María Elena left as naturally as she had arrived.

Realizing her image had reduced the boys to a state of anxiety, with that perfume of healthy earth promising the abundant harvest still surrounding them, the sharpener proceeded to give his first lesson in what he called "the happenings between man and woman and how we arrived to our planet." During the course of his lecture, he also said that masturbation was not a sin or abnormal, contrary to everything taught in catechism, and that to do it would not create a hunchback or drain the mind as several of the boys had been told at home, a bit of information that took an enormous weight off most of the boys.

Later in the day, news about the sharpener corrupting the children reached the ears of the mothers of the neighborhood. They became aware by means of the spying activities rendered by Augustico who years later became the most notorious "queen" of the Antioquian capital but who, at that young age did nothing else but carry the most awful news he could find to his mother, Doña Carlina, to make her hair stand on end. He told her now with a challenging urgency, "Mother dear if only you knew what that sharpener taught us today saying we could play with our wee-wees as much as we liked because it's neither a sin nor does it hurt anyone and that babies are not born out of the stomachs of their mothers or brought down from Heaven by the stork as you told me but they come out from a little further down—oh how horrible how dreadful mother and is that true?—and that hunchbacks are not degenerates. And he also taught us the difference between a burro, a mule and a horse."

Immediately, Augustico's mother, infuriated and shaking all over, rushed to the home of her neighbor, Doña Rafaela, to give her the news that this pervert was trying to steal the souls of the children and take them to the very bowels of Hell, wanting to denounce him before the authorities and prevent him from filling the heads of the poor innocents with such heretical, Masonic and communist ideas.

On the following Saturday, the bad luck which had trapped him in an undefended trench in the streets of Granada during the last hours of the Spanish Civil War, fell upon him again in the streets of the remote tropical city of Medellín, in the form of a committee of ladies dressed in black and armed with a priest and a policeman. The leaders were Doña Carlina and Doña Rafaela, followed by a half dozen curious ladies.

Even though the unexpected attack caught the sharpener by surprise, it gave the children ample opportunity to observe firsthand how he put into action one of the maxims he borrowed from Machiavelli: "To conquer, you must divide the adversary." Before they had time to address him he yelled, "Today, we're going to review multiplication tables starting with number five: five times one is five, five times two is ten, five times three is fifteen...." Looking straight at Doña Ofelia, Hernán's mother, a lady who was very practical and loved by everyone because of her liberal ways, he added, "And if you learn to multiply up to twenty by memory you will save half a year of life which otherwise you would spend figuring with paper and pencil. This will give you an enormous advantage in the commercial world."

As a good Antioquian, Doña Ofelia immediately understood the value of such teaching, hoping Hernán would some day take the reins of the corner grocery store which her husband, Don Emilio, consistently maintained at the edge of bankruptcy. She opposed the other mothers and gathered the support of Lenke and the Russians' mother, Doña Gutya, neither of whom could understand half of what was being discussed. But they joined in defense of the sharpener. Doña Carlina and Doña Rafaela insisted he never teach again and confine himself to his work, leaving the schools and the clergy in charge of the education of their children, but Doña Ofelia protested: "Even if my Hernán could only learn the first five multiplication tables I would gladly give my permission. I see nothing wrong in knowing how to multiply."

At last the priest, who hadn't said a word, offering first his blessing upon all those present, proposed a compromise: "So that everyone will be happy, let him teach arithmetic but not religion."

After a great deal of bickering they agreed that the sharpener could teach arithmetic and higher forms of mathematics such as engineering, physics, geology and astronomy, beside other sciences which used numbers more or less exactly, but that he must avoid any of the many theologies or psychology, which was the study of the soul. He was especially forbidden to teach sexuality, atheism, the occult arts—including any form of magic—Freemasonry or communism. Hypnosis was definitely out!

The policeman had not been able to take his eyes off María Elena during the debate. But he emerged half-dazed from his reverie, as someone who is rudely awakened from a profound and profane dream, when they asked him if he would render his official services to the compromise reached as arbiter and witness. "Arbitness?" he stuttered in confusion. And trying to recover, he added emphatically, "This thing's got to be fixed once and for all!" When the rules for the sharpener's conduct were established, the ladies walked away thinking they had won.

After the censorship began, the sharpener recreated the most basic scientific experiments and impersonated the great historical figures of the world from the antiquity of Greece and Rome to modern times, parading his heroes in majestic procession by the corner of the Avenida Echeverry and the little street of El Chumbimbo.

In the tropical winter, when the rains poured down for two months and the city was inundated, three canoes on a salvaging mission on the shores of the swollen La Loca stream were transformed in the eyes of the children as the sharpener turned them into the three caravels of Christopher Columbus on his first voyage to the New World. And as the mud overwhelmed the streets and the winds tore down the telephone posts, the sharpener became Magellan in his circumnavigation of the globe, with Captain Hernán Mejía's sure hand at the rudder, First Mate Abrahán Ostrovski, Second Mate Vladimir Ostrovski and Ensign David Rosenfeld climbing the slippery high masts, symbolized by the pisser trees, to look out for the dangerous reefs as they narrowly escaped the straits of Tierra del Fuego in their undaunted conquest of the seas.

In that corner so hidden from the rest of the world, the sharpener shared with the children the noblest happenings in history. He showed them the laboratories of Pasteur, Koch, Newton, Galileo, and of the Curies and transformed the Avenida into the placid garden of Mendel, showing them how that humble colossus formulated in secret "the principles of genetics." He made it possible for the children to meet, without hesitations or fears, man to man, Tolstoi and Lincoln, Leonardo and Simón Bolívar, Victor Hugo and Beethoven, Michaelangelo and Cervantes, Nostradamus! Atahualpa! Moctezuma!

He placed those who listened to him in contact with the past, the present and the future—with sparks bursting aroung him—while he polished and cleaned without ceasing, eliminating the rust that corroded and spoiled. From the green box mounted on his tricycle he took out—much like a magician—maps, dictionaries, reprints of famous paintings, weights and thermometers.

Frequently his tool box yielded an old gramophone, and then

symphonic orchestras from distant cities and the beautiful operas from remote concert halls filled the air with their stirring music. Often he presented, without commentary, excerpts from literature.

As the sharpener read, the children's circle of friends and people they knew expanded: One cloudy day, a fight ensued between two drunk cattlemen who had come down on horseback from the mountain, but the children saw El Chumbimbo transformed into La Mancha and the valiant Don Quijote—the gentleman of the sad figure who lived as a madman and died sane—mounted on Rocinante, vindicate his honor when he conducted and finalized the stupendous battle with the gallant and furious Viscaine.

When a suitor in frantic search of María Elena was captured climbing the balcony at Hernán's home, the children saw Romeo chasing his Juliet.

The drunkards at the corner cantina looked like the brothers Karamazov; the globes elevated during Christmas might travel to Julius Verne's moon; each miserable beggar walking across the neighborhood became Jean Valjean; the children played pretending to be Tom Sawyer, or the Lazarillo de Tormes, or Oliver Twist; each foul buzzard making the rounds of Medellín's skies was no less than Edgar Allan Poe's heartless raven and any mangy dog that strayed by the Avenida was Jack London's son of the wolf.

Three years of discoveries passed until the day when all that grotesque machinery of prohibitions and forced compromises was brought to the ground forever. The sharpener dismantled the perfidious contraption before his disciples so they would never forget how to get rid of a yoke: "The promises made to tyrants must never be kept!" he told them that Saturday which none of them suspected would be his last. And taking out an envelope from his vest pocket he said he had taught everything he knew and that the rest was up to them. He then opened the envelope and gave each of his little friends a large postage stamp of magnificent colors printed in Spain in 1928. On it was the picture of a sultry, beautiful woman who was completely naked, lying seductively on a couch, smiling invitingly, her eyes cast immodestly upon the viewer, the Maja Nude painted by Francisco Goya y Lucientes. It was the sharpener's good-bye gift: "Appreciate nakedness in art. When Goya painted the Duchess of Alba like this, he showed that a queen and a poor peasant are equal in their natural beauty. We must eliminate differences among social classes so we can all be free!" He added that his fondest hope was for Spain to get rid of its tyrant, General Francisco Franco.

All the neighborhood youngsters appreciated the stamp except Augustico who kept looking at the naked woman aghast. "This is sinful for sure," he mumbled. "With this you can get to Hell."

The sharpener overheard Augustico's remark and, looking out a little sadly, said, "I swear by my mother who's buried in Sevilla; I swear by my beloved Spain that neither Heaven nor Purgatory nor Hell exist. They are only inventions to frighten children and the poor so they can be controlled."

His revolutionary words did not take long to reach the ears of the whole neighborhood. Doña Carlina and Doña Rafaela, with a new committee formed with the backing of the curia demanded the sharpener's license be immediately confiscated.

After that day, the children never saw the sharpener again. No one knew for certain where he went. Some people said he was in another city sharpening; others believed he had returned to Spain to fight for freedom or that he had joined a revolutionary movement in one of the Latin American countries.

He left a void in the lives of the children. It took Chucho's grandmother, Doña Raquel's wisdom, to make it easier for them. One day, David and Hernán brought her a few gifts from their mothers, and she offered them corn bread and brown sugar water, saying to them, "I hear you boys in the Avenida are sad over the loss of your friend, the sharpener, upset you couldn't thank him for all he taught you before he disappeared. You shouldn't worry about it."

"It's just that we wish we could have said good-bye to him," Hernán said in a low voice.

"Oh, I see," she said, looking into the small flame of her cooking stove. "Then, you're fortunate, Hernán, because all goodbyes are a rehearsal of our own death and what the sharpener taught was how to live."

The poker players

Every Saturday evening my parents had a poker party at the house. The few Hungarians in the city played from dusk till past midnight. I was only an observer, since the adults wouldn't play with a youngster.

My mother played but often asked for timeouts to bring the food and drinks. She was also in charge of the corn kernels. Usually, there were eight players, including my parents, so my mother would count two hundred kernels of corn for each player before the guests arrived and place each mound separately on the tables. It wasn't a very precise count, but nobody ever questioned its accuracy or said they had been shortchanged. They accepted her accounting: "I made a count of the first two hundred kernels, four handfuls, and that's what each of you gets, four handfuls."

Sometimes my little brother Peter would take some of the kernels off the table and munch on them or push them up his nose before the guests arrived. One of us would scold him, "Leave it alone, Peter, that's for the grown-ups to play poker tonight. And don't put them in your nose!"

One of the poker players was a war veteran of the African desert, a mercenary of gigantic stature who blinked repeatedly. The sound of bullets exploding nearby had left him nervous for the rest of his days. He was a habitual poker player who spent most of his earned and borrowed money playing at some of the disreputable gambling establishments of the city. András Engel was his name. He had looked up my father to borrow money from him. That was one of his least successful endeavors while he was in our city, since my father barely had the money to keep us going. Engel was the only one who did not show up consistently at the Saturday evening poker games because there were more interesting ones in town, where they played for money. A professional gambler who bet high stakes in the casinos and gambling dens of the slums, called by many "mughouses," he won all the corn my mother put on the table. Engel had left Hungary when he was an adolescent and spent a tour of duty—some six years of his life—in the French Foreign Legion before coming to Colombia. He was full of tales of harrowing and morbid experiences.

"You think Engel will show up tonight?" Anyu—which is the name all Hungarian mothers are called by their children—would inquire from Apu, who was my father.

"He'll come if he has no money to gamble," my father would reply, rearranging some of the mounds of maize on the table that Peter had messed up. "Playing for corn kernels bores Engel."

"What you expect? He's a pro and we're just amateurs."

The one who had started the custom of playing poker at my home was not Engel. The first one was József Abramovits—Don José—as he became known in town. Mr. Abramovits to me, was a metallurgical engineer who specialized in restarting the productivity of abandoned gold mines and refining gold. He arrived in our city after my family had settled there and showed up at my father's shop. Dad sold wool, a difficult business that didn't yield much since we lived in the hot tropics. I was there, helping Apu after school, when Mr. Abramovits first came into our lives.

"I am in this city," he said by way of introduction, "in search of a fellow countryman who might help me get oriented. You must be Rosenfeld Imre," he addressed my father in Hungarian after he had taken a long look around the shop. "My name is Abramovits József." Hungarians always said their last names first.

Apu hadn't heard a word spoken by a stranger in his mother tongue in years and practically leaped to embrace the man. A quick and close friendship developed.

"I was told there was only one other Hungarian in town," Mr. Abramovits said, "so I came searching for you. I recognized your name. Were you the actor, the dancing comedian in Budapest?"

My father nodded his head, somewhat sadly. "Long ago," he said.

"And what in the world does an actor do here in this hot, God-forsaken place, selling wool?"

"Likely it is," my father answered with a deadpan, "we're both here for the same reason: to save our lives. With the war raging in Europe, I hear that Jews are, once again, not faring very well."

Mr. Abramovits entrusted my parents to find him a large house, with gardens and swimming pool, in the best part of the city, because he and his wife were planning to settle in Medellín in a month's time. "Find a really luxurious place," he said. "And tell the landlord I pay on a quarterly basis, with the first payment three months after we move in."

When my mother, who was supposed to find the house, heard about the payment clause, she was perplexed. "Nobody will rent you a big house unless you pay in advance."

"You don't understand the wealthy Latins, Lenke," he said to her. "The more eccentrically you behave, the more they are in awe of you, especially if you're a foreigner. I have to appeal to the wealthiest industrialists in this place and if I don't live at the best address, in the largest house, they won't support my enterprises." Mr. Abramovits was invited to stay with us for the brief time he was making arrangements in town. We had a spare room, usually used in the houses on our block for a maid, but since we couldn't afford one, the room was used for the occasional guest.

During his stay, Mr. Abramovits taught my parents how to play poker. Living with us for almost a week, he had plenty of opportunities to observe my brother Peter's behavior. The radio was the only object that aroused the child's curiosity. He played with the dials half the day and was particularly fascinated by the undulating noises of the static, the esoteric sounds of obscure dialects and the intermittent signals of coded messages in beeps. All these he began to imitate with uncanny accuracy.

"I think he might have a great radio career ahead," my mother speculated.

Mr. Abramovits looked at the child quizzically, shook his head and asked my parents, "How old is little Peter?"

"Five…almost six," he was told. Anyu didn't like to talk about Peter and was usually evasive when questioned about him.

"Have you taken him to see a physician?" Mr. Abramovits wanted to know.

When he heard all the excuses offered by my parents, he lit his pipe and placed a reassuring hand on my mother's arm, saying nothing. But the next day, just before he left the house on his way to the gold exploration fields in the remote area by the headwaters of the Bagre and Porce rivers, he called my parents aside and said, "I'm very fond of you and your family after these days in your company and I would be remiss if I didn't tell you what is so difficult for you to accept: your son Peter is in serious trouble and you must take him to specialists who might be able to do something for him." I had told my parents the same thing after watching my brother staring for hours at the green eye that opened and closed on our RCA Victor radio, but they wouldn't listen to a fourteen-year-old. Now, they paid attention and took Peter to be examined. Anyu began to have terrible headaches, worrying about the boy and my father had to work harder to bring in the money to pay a clinic for a treatment procedure that was to last years.

A month later, Mr. Abramovits's wife, Böske, joined the group of poker players. And soon afterwards, Engel arrived in town and reluctantly came into the group, contemptuous though he was of the corn kernels, shoving them at the end of the games toward the middle of the table after accumulating the whole pile in front of him.

The city was growing and it needed telephone services installed. Mr. Patai was sent by the Swedish company Ericson to supervise the operation. He came into my father's store one morning and said, "I'm also Hungarian." From then on mainly my father spoke. Mr. Patai would mumble something or say "Ahaaa!" He was the silent type. During the four years it took to put our city in touch with the rest of the world through a telephone network, I heard him utter at most a dozen short sentences. Though he never missed a poker session, he only came to watch.

My father teased Mr. Patai. "Gyurikám," he said to Patai, calling him by his first name, "we know you must be sick and tired of chatting so much over the telephones that you say nothing the rest of the time, eh?"

Mr. Patai chuckled, sucked on his curved pipe, gave my father a mischievous, conspiratorial look and smiled. No words! We called him "the telephone man."

I liked Mrs. Abramovits and called her "Böske *néni.*" She'd bring me and my brother Peter our favorite chocolate bars every Saturday. She was the most beautiful woman I had ever seen. I wished with all my heart I had an aunt like her instead of the stingy ones who came to visit us from Bogotá and never brought anything.

Anyu found for Mr. Abramovits and his wife Böske one of the most luxurious houses in the city, at the top of palm decorated Bolivia Avenue, with a view of the Andean hills, servants's quarters, swimming pool and orchid gardens. It occupied half a square block and its monthly cost was more than what my parents paid in two years for renting our humble apartment on what we called Cucaracha Street.

When the Abramovits couple arrived, they asked my parents if they had a spare mattress, two chairs they could borrow and some dishes. They were stark broke and had nothing to move into their palace. My mother was astounded. "How can you have the audacity to move into such a place and own nothing?" she asked.

"Our problems are not about pennies," Mr. Abramovits answered her. "They are with millions! The prominent address is what impresses people. In two months of gold explorations I'll have enough to buy any house we want and have my Böske fill it with the best imported furniture from Sweden, after I find the gold. Until then your mattress will do."

When Engel didn't show up at the gambling meetings on Saturdays, it was usually Mr. Abramovits who walked away with the corn kernels. He didn't take them home, of course. Nobody did. They played with the same old bunch of corn kernels for years, most of them having spent some time in Peter's nose.

My cousin Willie was the next member of the poker players. He and his family had made a timely exit from Hungary into Switzerland just before the doors of escape from the oncoming madness of war were closed. They settled in Bogotá, but Willie got bored because of the cold weather and constant rain and moved down the valley to the paradise of Medellín. Small and garrulous, often making off-color jokes and inappropriate remarks, he found it difficult to get hired. While he searched for a job, he ate at our home and slept in a cheap boarding house. After a few weeks, the Jewish community helped him get a job with one of the leading industrialists in town, a textile manufacturer.

Willie insisted he had an advanced degree in biochemistry, earned in Hungary, but as the days went by, his skills in the laboratory provoked serious doubt, and he was assigned to washing test tubes and doing other menial tasks. Willie was a clever young man, I thought, because he taught me a few wrestling holds and boxing techniques. A frail boy, I could use every bit of help in defending myself from the bullies of the neighborhood. But I found out that Willie wasn't really so smart, although he was good at talking up a storm. I never saw him win a single poker game and he was usually the first to lose all his corn kernels. Willie couldn't even beat my mother, who didn't have the vaguest notion about cards.

Willie's fondest wish was to own a car and, after working at the lab for a year, he purchased a beat-up model T Ford which he constantly polished. One Saturday afternoon, he came by our apartment before the poker game began, and drove several times around the block where we lived, attracting everyone's attention by honking and speeding. Finally, he parked the shiny little car in front of our building as he leaned on the horn. He invited me for a ride and —without consulting me—drove to Lovaina, the well known red-light district in the city.

I had heard of it and knew its whereabouts, but had never been there. When I realized with trepidation where he was taking me, he said, "Don't get spooked, they won't bite you. Most of the *putas* are not working yet."

"Oh," I said, somewhat dazed, not knowing what to say. "I didn't know that!"

"They're taking their baths, getting ready for the evening. I'm going to take you to the best whore house in town. I'm well known there. Wait and see what a nice bunch of girls they are."

When we arrived in the district, Willie drove as he had in our neighborhood, honking and speeding, screeching his brakes until half the women who worked came out of their houses, wondering about the commotion. He waved to them and yelled, "Anybody want ride?" He spoke Spanish very poorly, with a thick Hungarian accent and, although the women giggled and some of them touched the car, none of them wanted a ride. Not getting the kind of attention he sought, Willie drove to one of the larger houses, over the lawn, stopping in front of the open door, barely leaving enough space for a person to wedge through. Several of the women, wearing only brassieres and panties, came to look.

I was so embarrassed I wanted to hide, especially when I heard one of the women remark, "Oh, it's that stupid foreigner." But a couple of them lingered by the car, admiring its shine, exaggerating its merits.

"See? Didn't I tell you they'd go for it?" Willie asked, nudging me. His face was flushed with pride. He got out and embraced one of the women, patting her behind, tickling her until she began to wiggle out of his clutch.

"Come and meet my little cousin," he said, pulling two of them by their arms. They came over to me, smiling. "*Hola, muchacho*! Oh, he's adorable, Willie," they teased. "Now, if only you were this nice we'd really put out for you." They left me alone when they saw my discomfort.

By the time Willie took me back home, my father had arrived from his work. "I took the kid over to see the *putas*," Willie announced to my parents, "but he wasn't too interested. Maybe in another year or two, eh?" he added, turning to me, pushing his elbow into my ribs and feigning a jab to my chin.

"Is your head so soft you have no sense at all, Willie?" My mother was angry at him. "Are you trying to pervert our child? Never take him there again! And don't talk about whores when you're in my house! Or say vulgarities!" My mother could be a tough cookie.

After my father admired the Ford, Willie asked him if he wished to have a driving lesson before the poker games began.

"Sure, I'd like to learn," my father answered. "Maybe someday I'll have a car too."

While we ate, Willie showed my father how to drive. On paper. After dinner, they studied sketches of the car's driving mechanism drawn by Willie until my father was able to explain step by step how to shift from gear to gear.

"This is too easy," my father announced. "Teach me how to go in reverse, Willie."

"Reverse? We should actually go to the car now and put into practice what you've learned on paper, Uncle Imre. Reverse is the last lesson."

"Well, I'm ready to learn about reverse."

"I guess you're still a comedian, Uncle," Willie said. He proceeded to explain the reverse mechanism hesitantly, wondering what my father was up to.

While my mother began preparations for the poker game that was to begin in a couple of hours, I followed my cousin and Dad to the car and slid into the rumble seat without being invited. Willie drove to a park with ample driving space where La Loca, a stream that surfaced from under the houses out into the street, meandered for two blocks before being channeled under the huge cathedral that was the local tourist attraction.

"Okay, Uncle, I'll turn off the ignition key. Get in the driver's seat and start from the very beginning," said Willie, fixing his eyes on my father as though he were warning him not to exceed the speed limit.

My father sat behind the wheel and announced: "I still say it's too easy forward. I'm going into reverse."

"Wait a minute, Uncle," Willie protested. "I thought you were just kidding me about the reverse business, making a joke. A person starts the first lesson forward, not in reverse."

"Didn't I explain reverse the way you taught me, Willie?"

"Yes, you did, on paper. But you have to get a feel for the driving at first, Uncle, and if it goes well forward you can try it in reverse. Reverse is left for later, after you know how to drive forward."

"Well, this forward driving is too elementary, Willie. I'm going to show you I can do it backwards first."

"Uncle, what will you give me if I let you do it?" Willie was usually out to get whatever he could.

"I'll set you up with a couple of beers during the poker games, besides the dinner you already ate," Apu hedged and then said reassuring the young man, "If anything goes wrong, you take over, Willie. You're sitting right next to me, aren't you?"

From the rumble seat, I watched the proceedings, looking from one to the other as they talked. "Will you teach me how to drive, Willie?" I inquired. "I'll do it forward first."

"You're too young," my father said, as he turned on the ignition key.

Amazingly, my father was able to keep the motor running and smoothly put the car in reverse, but the speed went up very quickly while Willie screamed, "Slow down, lift your foot!" His warning came too late. The car moved backward at great velocity and ran straight down the embankment of La Loca, landing in the middle of the stream where the motor died. People came to watch, standing on both sides of the creek, and as my father, Willie and I stepped out of the car into the polluted water, we were rewarded with a prolonged round of applause from all the curiosity seekers. It was the last time that my father drove a car.

Another couple, recently arrived refugees from Hungary, Jancsi and Czunczi Schréter, joined the poker players. Jancsi found employment as head technician at the recently established leather tanning plant founded by a Russian emigrant from Siberia. Jancsi had a doctorate in chemistry, but didn't know anything about tanning leather. He came to the poker club, as it was being called, and everybody worried whether a thousand skins from recently slaughtered cows and bulls would be properly tanned since Jancsi's only knowledge about tanning came from a book he read at the local university's library. For two weeks the poker players fretted, not knowing whether Jancsi would be able to keep his job. On the third Saturday, by the time all the skins had been taken out of the tanks where they had been submerged in acid, Jancsi was in his glory, announcing to everybody, "You can relax! All the skins came out beautifully tanned." My father opened a bottle of champagne he had been saving for a special occasion and all the poker players toasted Jancsi's success. But still, it was his wife, Czunczi, who attracted most of the attention. She was a tall, statuesque blonde, with ample breasts that heaved as she breathed, who kept repainting her large mouth with new coats of lipstick instead of paying attention to the card game being taught to her.

Until the Schréters joined the group, there had been a kind of predictable rhythm to the poker sessions. The participants drank and ate and smoked in the midst of lively conversation, sometimes talking about the war in Europe and the fate of the Jews, everyone resigned to losing to Engel. I figured it was Czunczi's presence that introduced tension to their sessions. The men in the group behaved strangely in her presence, excepting Patai, who just kept silent, and my father, who had told me that during his many years on the stage he had learned to ignore women like Czunczi. I was sure of it when I looked up and saw Patai acknowledge my own discovery as he smiled at me mischievously, nodding his head. He knew more than I did about what was happening in the group.

I witnessed the moment one evening when Mr. Abramovits, playing opposite Czunczi, took a deep look into the depths of her pale blue eyes, sending a shudder of passion through her that would not abate. His wife, Böske *néni*, noticed and blushed as she looked away.

My mother, in charge of the evening's activities, sensed what was going on and tried in vain to separate them, but Czunczi and Mr. Abramovits did not try to conceal their lust for each other.

Another love interest sparked as the members of the poker club followed with intense curiosity the reports given by Willie regarding his love affair with a Romanian girl. Eliza was all Willie could talk about. The poker club members were surprised when they heard about Eliza's family's demands. Willie was so embarrassed, he could hardly pay attention to the poker game as he explained the details.

As it happened, the parents of the young woman didn't trust Willie when he asked for her hand in marriage. They were Orthodox Jews with a prosperous furniture business. Salomón Lebovits, the girl's father, took Willie aside and confronted him with the question that seemed to bother Medellín's entire Jewish community: "We don't know what's with your family: they say that some are Protestants, some are Catholics. How do we know you're Jewish? I'm not letting my daughter marry a *goy*."

"My uncle in Bogotá converted to Catholicism, that's all. Ask me questions about our faith," Willie challenged. "I studied for my bar mitzvah in Budapest. Write there and find out from the rabbi."

Salomón shook his head and tugged on his beard. He took off his glasses and cleaned them. When he put them on, he looked at Willie as though he had never seen him before. "I don't know what kind of a Jew you are with Catholic or Protestant relatives. There's something wrong! I need more proof and we can't get in touch now with any rabbi in Budapest."

Soon after these revelations by Willie, a delegation of elders from the Jewish community, most of them recent arrivals from Europe, came with him to see my father. They refused to enter our apartment and talked on the sidewalk. Since they knew that my father didn't speak Hebrew or Yiddish, they addressed him in Spanish. My father told them everything he knew about his family's religious background and assured them that both his sister Manci and her husband Maurice—Willie's parents—were Jews, descended from Jews on both sides of their families. Salomón listened carefully, taking notes and often consulting in a hushed voice and in Hebrew with the elders. "And you claim to be a Jew, but never attend a service, and your brother and his family converted to Catholicism. Is that it? Or was it Protestantism?" Salomón wanted my father to repeat all the details three or four times.

Neither Salomón nor the elders were satisfied. They huddled in a corner and resumed their intimate discussion for a while. When they arrived at an agreement, all of them nodded approval as though the wisest decision had been reached, Salomón came over to my father and Willie, saying: "You and Willie need to show us your penises and then we'll see if you have been properly circumcised or not."

My father was astonished. "The last person who wanted to check on my penis was a Nazi. You can take a long look at your future son-in-law's pecker if that's how you like to spend the time of day, but you're not going to get me in that position," he blurted out, laughing.

"Then he can't marry my daughter," Salomón answered impatiently. "We have to examine as many members of his family as possible. Who knows, maybe Willie is a Catholic too."

"Willie is a Jew and so am I. I guarantee it. Examine him, but why me? I'm not marrying your daughter. Examine his father if you must."

"He's in Bogotá. You're the only other adult male in his family here in Medellín. I'm sorry, Willie: no show, no wedding!"

Willie fidgeted nervously all along. "Uncle, for God's sake, what's the big deal! Show them what they want to see, for my sake. I love Eliza and want to marry her," he pled in Hungarian so the others wouldn't understand.

"Don't worry, Willie, you'll marry her, but I'm not going to display myself to these idiots."

I was standing by when I noticed Salomón slyly sashaying toward me, with a gleam in his eyes, made larger by his thick spectacles. He looked at me and pointed a finger in my direction while he turned his face toward the elders.

"Oh, no, not me, you don't!" I screamed and took off.

After much deliberation, they reached a compromise. They would examine Willie and have his father and brother fly in from Bogotá.

The elders stood in a tight circle in the middle of Cucaracha Street's sidewalk, where Willie disappeared from sight in their midst, privacy suddenly being a big concern. I returned from my wild escape and saw everything. Each one of the elders frowned intently while studying Willie's penis and asked him to move it so they could look at it from every angle, especially the underside. What they saw must have met with their approval because a few months later Willie and Eliza were married.

The members of the poker club toasted Willie on the night he passed his test until the young man got drunk and had to lie down before he fell down. They laughed all night and got friendly with each other as never before. Even the telephone man said a word of merriment. But the evening ended badly for the Abramovits's and the Schréters's when Böske found her husband and Czunczi kissing each other passionately behind one of the doors. Both Böske and Jancsi left the party early, but their spouses remained.

To ease the growing tension my father said, much like the comedian he had been, who overuses good jokes in a crisis: "Again, my dear Patai, you're chatting so much over those telephone wires you'd just as soon remain silent, but once in a while I'd like to know what's on your mind." Patai listened, smiling, enigmatic as always, and went on sucking his pipe.

The poker sessions continued and my mother was kept busy either admonishing Czunczi not to be so flagrantly provocative, since Böske Abramovits became Anyu's best friend, or trying to stop András Engel from recounting his experiences around the world where I could hear them, because they invariably ended in mayhem. I kept urging him on, fascinated by the man's life as a soldier of fortune. According to his account, he was not a stranger to any of the five continents nor the seven seas. Wherever he found himself, whether it was London, Bombay or Río de Janeiro, he could easily make a living. But not by gambling. Gambling was how he'd lose what he had gained working. Whenever he ran out of money, which was often, given his compulsive proclivities, he'd get some glue, a pair of small scissors, a few white pieces of cardboard and black paper. Standing in front of theaters or expensive clubs, he'd fix his gaze on anyone who might look like an easy target and in a matter of seconds cut out a profile from a piece of black paper and glue it on white cardboard, resulting in a little masterpiece portraying the finer features of the subject's silhouette.

As interested as I was in hearing Engel's stories I was nevertheless responsible for interrupting for nearly half a year his participation in the poker club. I became his employee; I got my very first job with the gambling artist. I worked for him for six and a half weeks. Then I quit and he fired me. I don't know which came first.

During a particularly altruistic stage in his life, Engel approached the British and American Red Cross and offered to collect money for them, to be used for their work with war casualties. He needed an assistant who'd carry a valise for him, filled with little posters of silhouettes of Winston Churchill's and Franklin D. Roosevelt's profiles, with a large "V" for Victory between them. He gave these details in front of the rest of the poker players and they all recommended me. He offered one peso a day and since I was determined to help the Allied cause, I accepted.

My father gave his permission readily but Anyu was reluctant to have me spend much time with the likes of Engel. "He's a nomad, an opportunist," she declared as they discussed the matter after everyone had left. "There's nothing a boy your age can learn from him." My father, on the other hand said, "Except he may learn something about life." "Yeah, but what kind of life, I'd like to know," she sneered. But she gave in since I wanted so badly to contribute to the war effort. "I would be practically employed by the Americans and the Brits to win the war against the damn Nazis," was my most convincing argument. The arrangement with the two Red Cross organizations was that Engel could keep thirty percent of the money collected. My cut was a daily peso.

Lacking other outlets to express their solidarity, the local defenders of Democracy dug deeply in their pockets and gave generously. Engel-tall and cunning, always impeccably dressed—looking like the patriarch of a respectable family, was a master at extracting money. He knew exactly what to say, what kind of a face he must make to elicit a greater donation. We'd enter a shop, me respectfully trailing Engel by a few paces. He'd ask for the person in charge. When the owner or manager of the establishment appeared, Engel said, "I represent the American and British Red Cross on behalf of the wounded soldiers of the war. Those who have sacrificed limb and life for our freedom in the world would appreciate a donation to help them get well. Please open your heart to them. And proudly display this sign." At that precise moment I'd pull out of the valise the Churchill and Roosevelt sign. His posters were displayed throughout the entire city in the windows of most of the stores. A few larger donations were made to him privately by some of the richest industrialists, but it was not at all certain whether he declared all the income received. My mother was sure he cheated. "He gambles," she said, "for money, not just for corn, and I don't trust gamblers."

As the days of the campaign unfolded, I got used to a schedule. Engel demanded that I dress in my best suit, arguing that contributors liked to give money to people who were well dressed, not to the paupers who really needed it. "People only give loose change to beggars," he'd say, blinking. "We want big checks for the Allies."

I woke Engel every morning at nine and then waited at the hotel's restaurant for him. There, Engel had a leisurely breakfast while he read the paper. We set out on our mission before ten. He had a map of the city and we systematically covered every business sector. At noon, we rested since no one worked at that hour of the siesta, had lunch—which was one of my perks—and then worked the businesses from two to five in the afternoon.

Around three o'clock every day Engel disappeared for an hour in the most disreputable slum in the city, Guayaquil. He'd usually leave me drinking a soda in a bar like The Black Dog, Venus's Cradle or The Pharaoh. Even at that time of the day the music from the juke boxes was deafening, playing tangos and boleros. Transient characters scrutinized me with sometimes threatening looks as I held on to Engel's black valise full of victory posters and receipts.

Tired of the long wait one day and fairly certain that my boss was gambling somewhere in the vicinity, I made inquiries and went searching for him in dark, smoke-filled rooms in several gambling establishments that were hidden from public view. I finally found the gambler on the third floor of the Guayaquil Drug Store, where the poker stakes were high and wounded men were often carried out on stretchers to the San Vicente Hospital.

Engel, his coat over the back of his chair, a large cigar sticking out of his mouth, his shirt sleeves rolled up, sat sweating, with a pile of money on the table in front of him, his pockets bulging.

When Engel saw me, he was obviously relieved. "Am I glad to see you," he said to me in Hungarian. "Today is my lucky day! I'm four big ones ahead!"

"Four big ones? Four?" I asked, looking at his pile of money, not understanding.

"Yes, four, you dummy! Four thousand!"

He began to count the bigger bills. "I'm giving you two thousand pesos to keep for me until after the week-end. And listen to me carefully: you have to promise me that no matter what I say to you between now and next Monday morning, you won't give me any of this money back. Understand? I want it available to pay major debts on Monday. I'm afraid I'll gamble it away if I keep it with me. So remember, no matter what I say or do, hang on to the money until Monday. Now, get out of here fast, before someone takes it away from you!"

The next day was Saturday, when we usually worked only during the morning hours, even though I got a full peso for my efforts. I can't say my boss—"the Sahara desert killer," as my mother called him—wasn't generous!

I showed up as usual at Engel's hotel. When he came down for breakfast he was bleary-eyed and worn out. "I think we'll skip work today," he said to me, rather anxiously. "But here's your peso anyway. Now, where is my money?"

"Don't worry about your money, Engel *úr*, sir, it's in a safe place."

"I want it now!"

"You ordered me not to let you have the money back until Monday morning."

"Forget about that, boy. I'm asking you to give it all back. I need it this very afternoon." Engel's face twitched.

I stood in front of Engel, wetting my dry lips, screwing up my courage to confront the tall, strong veteran of the African wars. "Engel *úr*," I said, resolutely, "your money is safe and you'll get it back Monday, first thing in the morning. Just as we said, as you told me several times. I promised and I'll keep my promise."

Engel turned red and clinched his fists. He was still having difficulty opening one of his eyes and blinked fiercely. He mumbled an obscenity in French that I could not understand, though our French teacher—*Monsieur Pancho Castro*—at the Liceo High School had taken timeout to teach us a few vulgarities that might come in handy in France. "I'm coming over to your home and I will have your parents find the money," Engel warned me, clenching his enormous fist before my face.

Now, I blinked. "They can search all they want, they won't find it. I put it where nobody can find it. But you'll get your money on Monday, day after tomorrow. I'm not one to go back on my word."

"You're a stubborn little brat! You get that money to me right away or I'm going over to your parents."

"Why don't you wait till this evening, when you'll be there anyway and take it up with all the poker players. I think they'll agree it's important to keep one's sworn promise."

"Don't give me any more mimicaca! If you don't go and get that money—my money—right away, I'm going to the Police! Right now, take me to the money!" He was furious.

Finally I blurted out what had been stuck in my throat all along: "I don't think either my parents or the Police would like it if they knew you're gambling with Red Cross money. And I don't care if I lose my job!"

"You're fired! Bastard!"

Next Monday morning, I went to the hotel with Engel's money in an envelope wrapped with heavy tape. Engel opened the envelope and saw the money was there. "Good boy!" he said, "here's twenty pesos for your troubles. Sorry I gave you such a hard time. And you're not fired." The twenty pesos—in those days on a par with dollars— was a lot of money for a boy.

I refused the money. Instead, I handed over the briefcase and told the astonished Engel, "I'm very sorry, Engel *úr*, but I can't continue working for you. I'm on my way to the United States and British Red Cross agencies to inform them you gamble away the money that's supposed to go for the war casualties. I thought you should hear it from me first."

Engel stammered in disbelief as the blinking got revved up. "Have you gone mad, boy? You don't know anything about it. There are receipts I hand in every day. You want to ruin me?" I shrugged my shoulders and left. I didn't see Engel again until months later, when he appeared in the city again, organizing an exposition of European paintings, only a few of which were authentic. He rejoined the Saturday eve poker players at my home and nobody said anything about our previous encounter. I had, after all, lacked the courage to denounce him.

When my parents asked me why I quit the job I merely said that Anyu was right and a gambler was not to be trusted. She was curious, asking for details, but I said nothing.

"Why don't you ever tell me anything?" she demanded to know. "You never trust your mother, only your father!"

"I trust you also, Anyu, but you worry about everything so much. And you get these terrible headaches when anything goes wrong, it's best not to tell you."

Her migraines had gotten worse through the years. They rendered her nearly helpless. Most of her distress was about Peter, who was lately urinating in his pants and unable to learn much in school. Her fears of a Nazi invasion and any bad news from Europe provoked blinding pains. Her friend Böske Abramovits's marital distresses, told to her with fits of sobs and cries of anguish, also affected her. Böske spent half her time at our house complaining about her husband's infidelity.

Beautiful though she was, Böske seemed to sense that her charms were no match for Czunczi's passions and that her husband was helpless putty in the hands of the tall blonde.

I overheard my mother telling Dad about what Böske had confided in her: When José Abramovits returned from one of his long trips to the gold mines, he found his wife looking more radiant than ever before, pretending to be in the gayest of moods. They became intimate and much to his dismay, he found a few bite marks on his wife's breasts and arms, all carefully self-inflicted but made to look like traces of someone's eager passion on her flesh. She was coy when he inquired about the bites, leaving him mad with jealousy, certain that she had a lover.

For a while Böske regained her husband's affections, but Czunczi offered such an overpowering attraction that it was impossible for Mr. Abramovits to resist her. Finally, in her desperation, Böske came to see my mother one afternoon and during the course of their conversation she showed a pistol.

"I'm going to shoot both of them," Böske threatened. My mother begged her not to use the pistol and promised to act as her intermediary. She went to Mr. Abramovits first but he laughed when she told him Böske would stop at nothing -including murder- to regain his love. "The only one I love is Böske," he replied flatly. "Don't you women know that a fling is only a fling, even if it lasts a while?"

My mother went to see Czunczi. At first she tried to persuade her gently to no avail. Then she told her, "Böske is ready to shoot you and I'm telling your husband before there's a tragedy. Jancsi is a good man. Even if you don't seem to care, he wouldn't want to see you dead."

"Some people just can't stand to see others having fun," Czunczi protested. "Go ahead and tell Jancsi. He already knows anyway and there's nothing he can do about it."

When my mother came back to Böske with the results of her failed negotiations, Böske looked at her watch and said, "This is the time they get together." She immediately got in her car and drove to Robledo, one of the outskirts of the city, and looked for them at a bathhouse called Playa Rica—the meeting place for lovers in Medellín—where she knew the couple met.

Brandishing her revolver, Böske barged into various rooms until she found the frightened lovers. Then she fired six bullets, managing to miss both of her targets, though one bullet grazed Czunczi's forehead—leaving a permanent scar.

"You can thank your lucky stars I have such poor aim," Böske screamed at them. "But I'm going to take lessons and next time I won't miss." There was no need. According to Czunczi she was tired of her lover anyway.

Six months later, Jancsi—a gentle and obliging man—became the first Hungarian to die in Medellín. At the Hospital San Vicente's typhoid fever pavilion, he pronounced his last words before closing his eyes forever. "I'm sorry, *Czunczikám*, if I was a disappointment to you," he mumbled before the handful of his compatriots from the poker club, including Böske and Mr. Abramovits, who came to say good-bye to him. "I forgive you but I'll ask you one thing before I die: please wait until I'm buried before you find another lover."

Shortly after Jancsi's death, the poker club disbanded. After saying about a dozen words in four years, Patai came one day, stayed a while, smiling and puffing away on his pipe, and when it was time to leave, he took out of his pockets a small gift for each of us in my family and said, "It was nice. Goodbye." We knew we'd never see him again. When my father asked him where he was going, he moved his head from side to side and shrugged his shoulders. Later, we found out from the telephone company that he had been transferred to Lima, Perú.

The Abramovits patched up their differences and opened a gold refinery business in Caracas, Venezuela. It was difficult for my mother and Böske to say goodbye to each other. They cried and promised to write letters for the rest of their lives, but the years had a way of blurring good intentions and memories. Böske tried to make up for the lack of letters and, knowing how crazy my mother was over dogs, she sent a big box airmail containing a beautiful puppy who became the family's pet for nearly twenty years. My mother, of course, gave it a Hungarian name: "*Emlék*," which means keepsake.

Czunczi disappeared shortly after her husband's death. For years, nobody in the growing Hungarian colony of Medellín knew of her whereabouts until one of the many refugees from the '56 revolution came with the news that he had met a woman living in squalor among narcotrafickers in one of the most remote provinces in the jungle, who said she had been born in Hungary. She was described as tall, heavy set, aging woman who still retained some of her beautiful features although she was marred by a scar on her forehead. The refugee said her name was Czunczi.

Willie and Eliza, as the fairy tale tells it, lived happily ever after in the same city, surrounded by their children, and years later, by many grandchildren.

My parents went to live back in the old country at the Odry nursing home for retired actors in Budapest. My father, before he died, was able to resume his artistic career and was cast to play a major role in a motion picture called "The friendly neighbor." My mother, after his death, came to live with me and my wife in the United States, where I settled down as a psychologist and sometimes writer. I live out my days by the placid waters of the Willamette river in a forest facing the snowy peaks of the Cascades. Shortly before my mother's death, when she was nearly 100 years old, she asked me to spread her ashes at the Warm Springs Indian Reservation because it reminded her of the old Transylvania, where she was born.

My little brother, Peter, is the only member of my family who stayed in Colombia. He is the oldest patient at the Hospital Neuropsiquiátrico Julio Manrique in the village of Sibaté, near Bogotá. He entered the hospital shortly after the poker club disbanded. I visit him every year.

The stamp collectors

After reading *El Conde de Montecristo*, David wanted to become a writer. For a while he walked around with a long pencil on his ear and a note book, telling nosy neighbors he descended from a long line of poets from Transylvania—his mother's ancestors.

Raúl, knowing David's wish, approached him one day: "Have you seen one of these ball point pens, David?"

David examined the colorful pen, feeling it was the most wonderful object he had ever held in his hands. "Where did you get this, Raúl?"

"My father's Chief of Detectives and confiscated it from a foreign smuggler, so there aren't any more of them around Medellín."

"Can I try it out?"

"Sure, write what you want. They never run out of ink."

David inscribed his name on a book he carried under his arm and marveled at the smooth flow of the writing. "Never in my whole life have I seen a pen like this, Raúl."

"I knew you'd like it. And I thought, since you're going to be a writer and I a football star, I'll trade you my pen for your International Football card collection."

After years of trading and maneuvering, David recently completed his colorful collection by getting the scarcest card depicting the king of the sport, the mighty Artur Friedenreich of Brazil, scoring his 1329th goal. He reached in his pocket and quickly handed over all fifty cards, lest Raúl change his mind.

The first use David made of his new pen was to copy word for word a poem called *Song of the Profound Life* he had discovered in an old book. He wanted to impress his parents and found an occasion to give it to his mother, Lenke. "I wrote this poem," he told her.

She read it slowly, often consulting her Spanish-Hungarian dictionary, becoming incredulous and ecstatic all at once. "Did you really write this, David? You're too young at eleven to write something like this."

"But I did write it, Mother," he waved his new pen in front of her.

"With this pen!" He lifted the bright object in front of her eyes.

Lenke took the poem over to Doña Carlina, who—as a high school teacher—knew about such matters, and came back a few minutes later, feeling humiliated.

That evening his father, Imre, told his son, "We want you to get started with this writer's notebook you've been carrying around by writing one hundred times with your new pen the following sentence in capital letters so you'll never forget a writer's first lesson: 'The author of the great Colombian literary masterpiece *Song of the Profound Life* is the poet Porfirio Barba-Jacob. I am sorry I plagiarized his work and swear never to do it again.' Then sign your complete name. You should never copy someone's work again, son. Never!" Lenke added an additional punishment of not letting him go to the matinee the following Sunday afternoon.

David's parents gave him the option of taking private lessons to study a foreign language or a musical instrument. He wanted both but they could afford only one. The teacher who taught guitar lessons, Don Eugenio—a chain smoker of cigars—was a dwarf hunchback, smaller than most of the adolescents who were his pupils. When he wasn't playing his guitar, he stood next to it, leaning on it, its neck extended just about even with his head. Most of the children shied away from him and he was only able to make a meager living by teaching in several schools. David chose English and the nearly blind and deaf octogenarian Englishman, Mr. Henry, who insisted on teaching out of Shakespeare and the Bible and was so boring that his students, including David, napped in his classes.

But the English lessons didn't last very long. Mr. Henry was an avid stamp collector and during one of his lectures, while he faced the blackboard, David took a large envelope full of stamps which Mr. Henry had recently received from England and hid it under his shirt. In spite of the crackling, Mr. Henry didn't notice anything.

After class, David walked over to his friend Hernan's home and called him out. "Hernán, look what a nice bunch of stamps I got from Mr. Henry."

They examined the collection. Most of the stamps had hundreds of duplicates. "He got these to trade," Hernán observed. "How did you get'em?"

"I took them while he wasn't looking. We could give them away to the kids in the gang. Everybody likes stamps!" They gave most of them away, feeling very generous.

Late that evening, Mrs. Henry, a matronly black woman, knocked at the Rosenfelds door. Lenke had met her before when she paid the monthly tuition fee for the English lessons.

Mrs. Henry came to the point immediately: "What I came to inform you is very embarrassing, señora Rosenfeld." She explained that a packet of valuable stamps had been taken from her home and the only person who had been there that morning was David.

"Oh, no, you must be wrong," Lenke said, feeling insulted. "David is such a studious and responsible boy, he couldn't have taken the stamps."

"Well, they were brought by the mailman just before David came this morning and they were gone right after he left the class. My husband interrupted his work on the collection to teach David. You tell me who else could have taken them!"

"I don't know but it wasn't my David."

"Your David had better answer for himself. I'm ready to call the police!"

Lenke went with Mrs. Henry searching the streets near the Avenida, leaving word that David should come home at once. When he showed up a few minutes later and saw from a distance Mrs. Henry's massive figure next to his mother, he knew instantly what was happening.

Before either Lenke or Mrs. Henry could say a word to him, he walked over to the black lady and said, "I am very sorry, Mrs. Henry, I took the stamps from Mr. Henry. I will never do it again."

Lenke might as well have been struck by lightning. "I can't believe my ears," she said. "You must be taking the blame for what some other boy did. Who did it?"

"*Anyukám*," he spoke to her in Hungarian, "don't make this any harder than it is. I did it. Nobody else did it, just me, by myself."

Lenke turned to him and slapped him across the face. "I'm ashamed of you: a son of mine, stealing. It's bad enough to have a son who can't learn anything -now I have a thief as well." She burst out crying.

Imre was appraised of the situation, shook the boy by his shoulders and demanded he return all the stamps. They walked into his bedroom and David brought out a small envelope containing the few stamps he had kept. "I gave them away but will get them back," David kept saying.

"These are next to nothing," Mrs. Henry said, when she was given the stamps and saw how few there were. "Out of two thousand stamps, this is all you're returning?" she asked, discouraged. A circle of neighbors and strangers gawking at them suddenly appeared in the empty street, magically conjured up by curiosity.

"Who did you give the stamps to?" Imre inquired impatiently. He wanted to spank David but remembered how badly he felt when his father beat him and his brother Mihály for stealing at the market place in Budapest and controlled his anger.

"I gave half of them to Hernán and most of the rest to the kids of the Avenida and the Chumbimbo."

"He'll get every stamp back to you, Mrs. Henry, before the week ends," Imre promised, while David kept saying, "I will, I will."

"I don't think you should be friends with Hernán anymore," Lenke said. "The two of you are always up to mischief. And he's not such a good student. What can you learn from him, the son of a grocer?"

"Mother: I'm the one who took the stamps, not Hernán. I gave him what I took. Don't blame him." She slapped him again, but David put his arm up to protect his face and she hurt her hand. She winced and David could hardly refrain from smiling.

Mrs. Henry left with the few stamps, unconvinced she would get the rest back. She turned around and threatened: "If you don't round up the two thousand stamps by tomorrow, I'll take you to the police."

"I'll get'em all back, Mrs. Henry. I just gave them away this afternoon. They're still around."

"We're coming with you, David," Imre said. "You'll have to explain your misconduct to the whole neighborhood, apologize to everyone."

It was quite dark at ten o'clock, when they began the recovery work, not the best time to go knocking at people's doors to retrieve stolen merchandise. They walked first to Hernán's home. The Mejías were in bed. Their maid came to the door and said the family had already retired for the night and that they should come back the next day.

"No," Lenke insisted, "tell them it's urgent. Tell them it's about a thief named David and his helper, Hernán." The maid looked at David with smiling eyes. "All right," she sighed, "I'll tell them: a thief and his helper."

Lenke briefed Ofelia. The two of them, followed by David, walked to Hernán's room which he shared with his brother Efraín, while Imre stayed outside, pacing on the sidewalk, smoking nervously. Hernán had heard what was going on and lay on his bed, pretending to be asleep with the covers up to his eyes.

"Don't play dead for me," doña Ofelia told him.

"What is it? What have I done now?" Hernán mumbled, feigning being awakened from a deep sleep.

She pulled the covers off his face. "C'mon, hand over the stamps."

Hernán got out of bed. He was wearing briefs and looked very thin and worried. "I got to get some sleep," he said, still pretending. "In this house nobody lets you sleep in peace."

"You'll go back to sleep as soon as you find every one of the stamps, not before. Don't pretend you don't know what's going on," Ofelia warned him. David held his breath, worried that Hernán might no longer have them.

"I've got this many," Hernán said, handing over the original crackling packet that was on a chair. "I gave some of my share to my brothers and sister."

Efraín got up and pulled out a big box from under his bed. "Here are the ones I got," he said, handing them over. Augusto, only six years old, slept through the ordeal. "I know where Augusto put his," Efraín said and he went to retrieve them.

They walked toward their sister Blanca's room. She had not missed a word since Lenke had come into the house and, even though she was the oldest of the Mejía children, she was frightened and burst out into the corridor saying, "I didn't do it! I didn't do it! Here are the stamps that fellow Hernán gave me," as though she were unrelated to her own brother. By this time, Don Emilio—Hernán's father—came out with his reading glasses on, wrapped in a heavy robe, wearing high boots. He walked in the wrong direction, like in a daze, bumping into a stand with a vase that fell with a crash: "What's going on around here?"

Doña Ofelia looked at her husband and her son. She couldn't contain herself any longer and began to laugh so hard she had to sit down.

Lenke was startled. "This is serious matter, Ofelia. Do you think these two boys should continue their friendship?"

Ofelia pulled Lenke's arm and calmed down. "Lenke, my dear," she said, "there's nothing wrong with these young goats. And in answer to your question, no, we shouldn't break up their friendship. I wouldn't worry about these two. They'll turn out alright, you wait and see. It's the ones who never get in trouble I worry about. These two are tomorrow's promise."

Deep into the night, David went from house to house, accompanied by his parents, making amends, reclaiming the stamps. He woke up the Garcías who had recently moved in from the village of Fredonia to establish what turned out to be a very prosperous men's clothing store. Don Oliverio, the head of the household, a tall and strong man, upon hearing David's confession summoned his whole family out of bed so they could witness what was going on. When they were all assembled he said to them, "I want everybody to hear David because that's how a truly honorable boy should behave." As a reward he gave David a crisp one peso bill. Each one of the seven children, from the smallest one who hardly understood what was going on, to the tallest, stood in line with the stamps they had received and listened politely to the lecture on honesty delivered on the spot by their father.

It was past midnight and David was still missing some of the stamps. As much as he hated to do so, he had to knock at the door of the Arango family, to retrieve the large share he had donated to his friend Raúl, the son of Medellín's Chief of Detectives, Don Aureliano. The Chief came to the door, slightly tipsy since it was his custom to drink aguardiente every evening after work. "What's going on, David? Don't you know what time it is?" he asked.

"Well, sir, I stole some stamps, Don Aureliano, and gave a lot of them to Raúl—he had nothing to do with the robbery, I want you to know—but I need them back right away, before tomorrow, that's today already, I guess, it is past midnight, because if I don't, the person I took them from, Mr. Henry, will denounce me at the Police Department."

Bleary-eyed and sleepy, David returned the stamps to Mr. Henry early in the morning. The old man counted them carefully. "There are eighty seven missing," he said, "but you have shown the proper amount of repentance and I will not pursue the matter with the authorities."

"Thank you, Mr. Henry. I brought you a bunch of Hungarian stamps my mother collected. Choose as many as you think the eighty seven missing are worth." Mr. Henry gladly took David's Hungarian collection but the English classes were stopped.

The price of freedom

On one occasion while riding the train, Hernán and David decided to climb on top of one of the freight cars. Lying on coffee sacks, they fell asleep under the blazing sun and the constant swaying of the train. When they woke up, the train had already gone by Cisneros, where they were to take the train returning to the city.

"Now, we won't be able to get home until tomorrow evening. Such is life, our plans foiled by sleep," Hernán said.

"Our parents will worry to death, Hernán."

"Yeah, I can see Ofelia praying for us when we are not back this evening. But it won't kill her."

"I never saw the end of the line, Puerto Berrío, when my mother and I traveled up the Magdalena River. We stayed on the ship. She was too frightened to go anywhere."

"They say it's full of whores, more than in La Pintada," Hernán commented as though he were an expert on such matters.

Upon arrival in Puerto Berrío, they found they barely had the money to pay for third class tickets back to Medellín.

Wandering around the small port town with their long poles, they gawked at the painted women who began to take up their positions sitting in front of their rooms along the streets, their legs spread, smiling at strangers and calling out to them, their voices nearly drowned by the blaring music from the cantinas. The boys looked but wandered on.

Late in the afternoon, by the shore of the Magdalena, they met an Indian who gave them a ride across the river, very broad at that point, to the settlement of Puerto Olaya. They were no longer in Antioquia but in another province, Santander, and were enormously proud of themselves for having crossed a border.

"Bet you we're the first ones from the Avenida Echeverry gang to have reached across the Magdalena into another province," Hernán boasted.

"I'm still worried about our parents, Hernán."

"There's nothing we can do. We'll be back home tomorrow before a telegram could be delivered to them. I'll say this, David: We had better make the best of this situation and enjoy ourselves before the horrible nagging we'll get tomorrow."

The Indian took them to his shack which was by the river's edge and offered them a fish dinner. "You can pick some fruit in the garden while I clean the fish, if there are any caught in the net," he said. "If not, we'll all eat fruit."

They walked behind the hut and saw a young bull pasturing in a meadow. Hernán was compelled to take off his red shirt and taunt him: "C'mon, *toro*," he dared the frisky animal, shaking his shirt by its sleeves in the style of the famous matadors, "let's see your stuff!"

The bull eyed Hernán obliquely at first from the corner of his eye, digging his paws into the soft ground. Hernán took a step forward, his chin tucked in, each hand grabbing a sleeve of his shirt. The bull turned and stared straight on, lowering his head. It was eye to eye combat. Terror spread over Hernán when he saw the bull race toward him, but he stood rooted to the ground. The bull's horn brushed near him. David was definitely impressed: "Olé! Olé!" he shouted with great enthusiasm. "You're a fantastic bullfighter, Hernán! Let's see you make another pass!" Hernán continued to play matador and, at a safer distance, he knelt down once and exposed his bare chest to the bull.

Now the Indian and his children got excited. "He'll make a good bull for the ring when he grows bigger," the Indian said while David kept screaming "Ole, olé," every time the bull's thrust was outmaneuvered. Finally, Hernán tripped on some roots and as he was getting up the bull butted him in the rear, lifting him off the ground and throwing him into the bushes. The beast was ready to attack again when David picked up Hernán's shirt and drew the bull's attention away from his friend. The bull charged David, who ran in panic waving the shirt, hiding behind a tree just at the moment the bull tried to gore him.

"This bull is too fierce for you boys," the Indian told them. He calmly walked over to the young bull, patted him on the neck and retrieved the shirt which was tangled in the horns. The incident ended Hernán's ambitions to follow in the great Manolete's footsteps.

"You boys can stay here and sleep on the hammocks outside," the Indian invited them after they ate. I'll take you back before the train leaves in the morning. I have to return to Puerto Berrío at dawn."

"We'd be in real trouble if we missed the train tomorrow," Hernán informed him.

"I'll have you back before daybreak. Now, I have to build a bigger fire to keep mosquitos away because white people like you have a peculiar smell that attracts them." The Indian handed them two empty flour bags and added, "Put these over your heads while you sleep so the mosquitos won't bite you."

They slept in the garden with the white sacks over their heads, pretending at first they were ghosts. In the morning, David was glad he had covered his head because welts from mosquito bites were everywhere his skin was exposed.

"I got about fifty bites all over me," David told the Indian, "but none on my face."

"I don't have a single bite on me," Hernán bragged. "They never bite me. They like blood from foreigners like you." He laughed.

The man spoke to his wife who had not uttered a word to the boys and in a few minutes she brewed a thick substance which she brought to David. "Cover your bite sores with this," she told him. He did so and the itching stopped.

For breakfast, the boys ate sweetened water in a coconut shell with corn bread. It was still dark when the Indian brought them back to Puerto Berrío in his canoe. The boys, urging him to go faster, debated with him what time of day it might be. When they heard the shrill sound of the train's whistle announcing its departure, they knew it was six o'clock. From the solitude of the river they watched helplessly as the train in the distance slowly moved out of the village.

"Now we're in real trouble, Hernán. We'll have to wait yet another day," David lamented. "We shouldn't of gone across the river."

Hernán shook his head, frowning. "Live and learn," he muttered. "Let's go to the train station anyway. Sometimes they have freight trains to Medellín."

They went to inquire at the ticket office but even before they arrived the train dispatcher intercepted them. "Are your names Hernán Mejía Peláez and David Rosenfeld Bártfai?" he asked them, stumbling with difficulty over David's name.

"The very ones, my Captain," Hernán answered.

They were invited into the office and given coffee. They accepted the cigarettes offered them. "We've been on the look-out for you ever since yesterday," the station master told them. "A radio message with your description was received by the police. They're searching for you in every village between Medellín and Puerto Berrío. Someone saw you in town in the company of an Indian but then you disappeared." The station master radioed back, saying the two missing boys had been found and received instructions to put them up at the Hotel Magdalena and place them on the next train back to Medellín.

It was a luxurious hotel, looking like an old palace, with spacious rooms, marble columns, tennis courts and the grandest dining room the boys had ever seen, with elaborate furniture, and waiters in elegant, white uniforms.

When Hernán saw the dining room his eyes widened. Nudging David's ribs with his elbow he said in singsong fashion, "Today we're going to eat like two bishops!"

The hotel had the reputation of being one of the best lodgings in the country; located by the edge of the jungle it had a distinctly tropical and relaxed ambiance. The boys spent most of the day playing in the hotel's olympic size swimming pool near a waterfall, next to a large cage full of monkeys and a smaller one filled with parrots.

That evening, while they ate dinner, David asked Hernán: "Man, did you notice how cramped the monkeys and parrots were?"

"Like sardines in a can. I sure wouldn't like to be one of them."

"There were thirty monkeys and sixteen parrots. I counted them. And their cages aren't that big." David was trying to figure out how much space each animal had but gave up after a short while.

"It's a shame," Hernán said. "Those monkeys are used to their freedom in the jungle. How would people like it if the monkeys got a hold of them and locked them up in a crowded cage! Freedom is the only thing worth living for!"

"You're one hundred percent right, Hernán. Nobody should lose their freedom. It's the greatest part of life!"

"Freedom for all!" Hernán exulted, lifting his glass of water. "How would you like to be free in a jungle one day and be stuck in a cage the next?"

They ate in silence for a while, thinking about the animals in the cages. Above them, the whirling sound of several electrical fans was heard. David looked up from his plate and asked in hushed tones: "Or how would you like to be locked up in a cage one day and be free in a jungle the next?" He stopped eating and looked around, "I've got an idea, Hernán: the cages are easy to open."

Hernán brightened up: "Of course! Late tonight, when there's no one around, we'll free the prisoners!"

Early next morning, when they reached the dining room to have breakfast, they were surprised to see several of the monkeys they had freed, hanging from the chandeliers, doing stunts. Three of them were recaptured by the hotel attendants but the rest were back in the jungle. And all the parrots had flown the coop!

"I guess we're going back to our cages," Hernán said when they boarded the train. They looked at each other and laughed. They knew there would be one hell of a scolding awaiting them at the end of the trip, but were happy remembering how the animals had scrambled toward freedom when they had opened their cages during the night.

Two loves II

Every day, the students of the Liceo rushed out of the building after the porter, Arcilita, an old man with a mop of white hair, rang the five o'clock bell. They ran three blocks to watch the girls leave their school. The boys begged Arcilita to ring the bell one minute ahead of schedule so they could get to the Central Femenino school before the girls left. Always high on the strong coffee he drank daily out of three full thermos bottles, Arcilita was like a chronometer, unfailingly ringing the bell with his Parkinsonian shake at the precise moment when he was supposed to. Some of the students tampered with the clock, setting it two minutes forward but Arcilita found out and reset it. "If a woman won't wait for a man, she's not worth your troubles," he told the boys.

Most of the girls waited behind the iron fence of their school as though lying in ambush for the boys. After the boys from the Liceo arrived each afternoon, the girls came out by the big portal of the Central Femenino. For many of the high school students, boys and girls alike, it was the only worthwhile time of the day, the rest being a tedious wait to be patiently endured.

David stood with the other students from his school in a row. He came to see a girl about his own age whose family had recently moved into a house half a block up from where he lived on the Avenida Echeverry. Her name was Mariela Carvajal and she had such a charming way of smiling, a sweet look in her eyes, that David found his head swirling in confusion the first time she looked at him when she came out to the street the previous Saturday evening to get acquainted with everybody in the neighborhood. Instantly, she became the focus of most of the boys's conversations in the Avenida. Now he saw her as she came out and called her name. They walked together, much of the time in silence, pretending to be completely at ease.

Just when their conversation began to flow, David remembered he had to pick up Peter. "I have to pick up my little brother from his school, Mariela," David told her. "It's only half a block out of our way."

Mariela went along. Peter was waiting at the one room special school, holding his cupped hands close to his mouth, mumbling. He saw David with the girl and snickered.

Mariela looked at Peter and the other children in the room and her long eyelashes fluttered for a moment over her large green eyes. An ineffable, somewhat sad look, akin to pity, invaded her lovely face. David watched her intently to observe her reaction to his brother and he sensed compassion in Mariela instead of the fear or revulsion many others showed.

"He likes you, Mariela. I can tell," David said to her, while Peter ambled along by their side, still talking to himself.

"Mariela is my brother's girl friend," Peter said to her all of a sudden, awkwardly rubbing his hands together and twitching all over.

"One thing about Peter, Mariela, is that he says whatever pops into his head," David said very embarrassed.

"I don't mind," she answered, a faint smile on her lips. "Most people never dare say what they really think."

For a few months, David accompanied Mariela to her school. Every morning they met by the fountain at the park crowded with walnut trees. In the afternoons they stopped to get Peter. The other boys and girls in the Avenida, aware that a romance was taking place, gossiped about them. Her parents were strict and forbade Mariela to befriend any of the boys, including David. But she disobeyed and went out with him anyway.

One Sunday afternoon they sneaked together to the Teatro Olympia—a movie house out of the way— and were seen sitting very close to each other by one of Mariela's relatives, a meddlesome cousin who immediately told her parents. When Mariela returned in the early evening from the movie, her parents held her down and carried out, while she screamed and begged, what families in those days customarily did in Colombia to adolescent girls who were overly flirtatious: they cut her lovely brown hair that cascaded down her back in translucent waves and shaved her head.

To hide her barren head Mariela wore a colorful turban that gave her an exotic, Arabian look, and went out, not only with David, but with other boys as well. With her olive skin, dense eyebrows, deep-set eyes and womanly features blossoming with a tenacity that no parental prohibition could restrain, she was more beautiful than ever. Many of the mothers in the neighborhood disliked her, including David's mother.

"Mariela is a flirt who soon will fall into bad ways," she predicted while the family ate. "I don't want my son to be seen with a girl like that."

Throughout the remainder of the school year and the following Christmas vacation, which lasted three months, Mariela and David furtively saw each other every day. But when the new school year began, she was enrolled at the Colegio de la Presentación, a religious school where nuns kept a constant watch over every move the girls made. A bus came to pick her up in the mornings and delivered her home late in the afternoons.

David and Mariela continued their friendship surreptitiously. She'd drop him notes from her seat next to the window on the back of the bus where the supervising nun could not see her. Some of her girl-friends conspired to deliver his letters to her. For days he worked over his first love poem which he dedicated to her. He was putting the finishing touches on it when his mother, peeking over his shoulder, read some of it and began tormenting him, "Now you're throwing yourself over that silly girl, wasting your time instead of doing your chores."

David tore the poem to shreds so she could not finish reading it. "Don't bother me, Mother! You're always embarrassing me!"

"I thought you had stopped seeing Mariela. It's not good for youngsters to get so involved. You don't do your homework since you met this floozy."

Hot rage overwhelmed him. He had an urge to strike her. "Floozy? You don't know what you're talking about! Mariela is not a floozy! She's always kind to Peter —never makes fun of him the way most everybody else does. I don't care about homework. I just wish you'd leave me alone!"

David knew the exact route of Mariela's school bus, every stop it made between her home and her school. He knew it would take it three and a half minutes to round the block after picking her up and arrive at the corner of Argentina and Girardot streets where three girls in their blue and white uniforms would be waiting for it. One of them, Nuri Caycedo, a youngster full of mischief who eventually became a nun, served as their go-between and delivered notes and letters back and forth. Five minutes later, David and Mariela could catch a glimpse of each other two blocks away, after the bus had circled again picking up more students. At one of the stops by the Parque Bolívar on Ecuador Street, the bus usually waited three or four minutes for a group of eight girls who lived in the vicinity. It was at that stop that David often had a chance to talk to Mariela. They'd look longingly and exchange the letters they had written to each other since their last meeting. On a couple of occasions they managed to hold hands for a few seconds through the window, feeling truly transported to unsuspected heights.

One day, Nuri dropped David a piece of paper which he read anxiously, knowing in advance it contained disturbing news. The note said: "Mariela is no longer at our school. She's a boarding student at María Auxiliadora." María Auxiliadora was the strictest religious school in Medellín, with a convent atmosphere and barred windows, where the girls were forced to pray when they were not studying. She could not go home.

Friends who knew Mariela's family told David that after she was punished for a minor prank, she spilled a bottle of ink on a nun's habit. Her parents were notified and they immediately transferred her to the new school where she was cloistered. He went there, a few blocks from the Liceo, and loitered near the building which looked more like a prison than a school, knowing that he would not be able to see her through the high barred windows but perhaps she might see him. He went there at every opportunity, often cutting classes or sneaking out of the classroom after answering the roll call. He'd walk around the block of Mariela's school and stop from time to time to look at the grey building with its massive iron grills, its forbidding cemented façade.

On a drizzly afternoon, while he stared at one of the windows of the third floor, a sheet of white paper floated down in the breeze. His heart pounding with excitement and anticipation, he positioned himself under it and reached up, feeling all the more elated because something from her, without touching anything else, was about to come directly to him. He walked away with the note tucked under his shirt and took cover in the solitude of one of the less traveled side streets before reading what she had written: "I will never forget you, David. But my life is not mine. Others are molding my destiny. I will fight them but I know I can't win. Take care. Always your friend, Mariela."

David kept the note and read it over and over, his eyes filled with tears, realizing there was nothing he could do to help her. His predicament worsened when Mariela's family moved to Cali, taking her with them.

Finding refuge in poetry, David walked around the parks where he and Mariela had been together, often returning to her school. He'd sit on the steps of a garden nearby, memorizing the immortal verses of *Rimas* by Gustavo Adolfo Becquer, the somber love poem *Nocturno* of José Asunción Silva and finding kindred feelings in Rubén Darío's *Song of Autumn in Spring*: "Youth, divine treasure… you left and never returned! In vain I searched for the princess… Who was saddened by waiting…"

At school, he plunged into various activities, trying to chase away the loneliness he felt at losing his friend, attempting to make up for his brother's deficiencies, and organized with his classmates a hiking club with the pretentious name of *Centro Excursionista de la Universidad de Antioquia*. He persuaded his mother to let him go on many week-end excursions to villages throughout the province. She agreed as long as they kept out of jungles, which were frightening to her beyond reason. He didn't tell her where they went when the excursions included a jungle. The club named him its historian and he kept a diary and photographs of the club's activities. He enjoyed that, especially when they gave him an I. D. card with his picture, naming him correspondent with full journalistic rights in the province's affairs. He felt good about his accomplishments, but his restlessness and anguish over Mariela's fate and her disappearance from his life continued to disturb him. Nothing seemed to lift him from his despair, his frustration at not being able to see her again.

A new radio program held weekly at the prominent Voz de Antioquia became one of David's favorite events. Although the program was open to students of all the city's high schools, boys from the Liceo were the main participants. David usually chose to answer questions about Literature. Often his friends from the Avenida came to the radio station to cheer for him. After a few months, he became one of the members of a panel in the weekly program, never lacking for money to buy his favorite novels.

One Sunday morning, David, his best friend Hernán and the Ostrovski brothers, Abrahán and Vladimir, who also lived in his neighborhood, sat on a bench at the Parque Bolívar. While they listened to the open-air concert, Hernán made a suggestion: "How about going to a dating house this afternoon, fellows? I hate to see you three foreigners still cherries in my own country while I'm becoming a ripe old banana. This tropical country of mine has to live up to a reputation of not letting any boy over fifteen stay virgin!" Hernán had flunked out of the Liceo, run away from home and was the only boy in the Avenida who was making money, working at a mill. He had worldly experiences while away and for his daring he had earned the respect of every boy in the neighborhood.

That afternoon the four of them went to Lovaina, where the better dating and whore houses of the province were located. Hernán knew the territory and led them to a house slightly out of the main district, next to the Bosque de la Independencia, a wooded park with a lake offering boat rides and amusements.

The establishment Hernán selected was owned by one of the best known courtesans in the city, La Mona Platos, a very amiable and beautiful woman, blonde and somewhat plump, with a soft heart for students. She was especially generous with students of the Liceo, known to render her very good services on credit to the boys from that school. It was rumored that students from other schools had lied to her, claiming they too were Liceans, but she knew enough about the city's educational institutions to interview her young clients and find out the truth. Now, she stood by the front door smiling and said, "So you boys go to the Liceo? You take any courses from Don Bernardo?" She knew the names of all the teachers, some of whom were her customers. When she was convinced they were students from her favorite school, she said, "I can take good care of all four of you for three pesos each. I'll be ready in my room—second one to the left—in ten minutes. You boys arrange the order in which you want your stones unloaded."

They drew lots and Hernán won. "It's only fair," he said, "since it was my idea." David was to be second and Abrahán last. Vladimir, third, said something in Russian to his brother, who hardly ever said a word, and after that, the two brothers laughed with unrestrained glee for the remainder of the afternoon, before and after their encounter with La Mona Platos, but Hernán and David never found out what tickled their funny bones.

While Hernán was occupied and his other two friends were doubled over giggling as they waited their turn in the street, David heard a window shutter open and a woman's voice: "Young man, young man, come and talk to me." He was startled as he turned around, not seeing anyone. "Over here," the voice called out again as a small window opened slightly. "Don't be afraid, come and talk to me." David looked through the window and saw only darkness inside the room. Behind the iron bars, a brown skinned, faintly rouged face appeared, her large black eyes heavily penciled, her delicate fingers playing with her long black hair. When he moved closer she dropped a white shawl that half concealed her face and smiled, moving her full lips in a provocative way. David never saw a face like hers before.

"What a handsome young man you are," she said. "You must be a foreigner... North American? German?"

"Hungarian," David said, trying hard not to look away from her gaze.

"Oh," she exclaimed, smiling again. "From beyond the sea." She looked at him intensely, studying each one of his features. "You have a nice body," she said easily, as though she had known him for a long time. She looked at David with reassurance, sensing his reluctance, and asked, "Have you had any pleasures?"

David looked away from her, hesitating. "No," he said, "it's... it's... been Platonic."

"Oh, Platonic!" She laughed a little, tasting the word. "So you never touched a woman? You never held one in your arms?" She came closer to the barred window and let the shawl drop down her bare, smooth shoulders, as she opened her full mouth and slightly moved the tip of her tongue over the edge of her perfect row of upper teeth. "Did you ever kiss one?" she lowered her voice.

David took a deep breath and looked at her, feeling almost detached, as though his spirit were floating somewhere close but outside of his body, and shook his head: "I wanted to, but didn't have a chance."

"It's good that you wanted." She paused a while and then asked, playfully, "What's your name?"

"David, David Rosenfeld-Bártfai."

Now she looked at David in the eyes in a dreamy, ethereal way. He could have sworn he saw a moistness in her eyes.

"David," she whispered again, her lips wet, her long eyelashes almost closed, "would you like me to teach you?"

He answered quickly, eagerly, giving in to his fate: "Yes, I'd like to know, I'd like to."

"And will you come back if you like what I teach you? Will you come again to see me, David? Promise?"

"Yes, I promise I will, yes." His heart was pounding.

"We'll begin," she said softly, extending her bare arm through the iron bars and touching his face gently. She then placed her face between two of the iron bars and, pulling him close to her, gave him a long and hot kiss on the mouth. Then she said, "I'm ready for you."

After she stripped him of his awkwardness and they lay relaxing on her bed, he asked her name.

"María Duque," the tall, swarthy beauty said, "but my best friends call me Mariela."

Years later, David wrote a short story called *Two Loves*, where he told about the two Marielas in his life, the real one who was like a freely given but unattainable dream of joy that vanished with his youth's yearnings, and the unreal one who helped him step across the boundary of innocence through a purchased dream of silk and cinnamon into the reality of manhood. But he finished writing the story long before the full tragedy of his friend's fate became known to him.

Fifteen years after the story was published, David was invited back to Medellín to give a lecture at the province's institution for the emotionally disturbed, since he had become a specialist in the field of psychopathology. It was the same mental hospital where his brother Peter was confined as a patient for all those years, a place commonly referred to in Medellín as "*la casa de los locos*."

Later, after the lecture, David was taken to visit a luxurious institution for the wealthier classes, euphemistically called "a retreat" in the hills surrounding the city, close to the village of Rionegro. As he toured the facility he heard a woman's voice repeatedly wail in a most plaintive way, "*Mamacita, Mamacita, ¿por qué yo?*, why me? Why me? *Mamacita, Mamacita, ¿por qué yo?, ¿por qué yo?*"

His colleague said the woman spent hours repeating those few words and wanted David's opinion on the case. As he approached her, he recognized his first love. She was married to a prominent man and had three children, but the damages of childhood abuses she endured caught up with her, transformed into a pent-up fury unleashed against herself in a second suicidal attempt. Her hair had strands of grey but was well kept. For a moment David forgot all his training and vast experience in clinical objectivity. They embraced and she gave him the faint smile that emerged from the confusion of her sadness before the startled physicians and nurses. But there was nothing David could do to help her, even though he spent hours consulting on her behalf with the psychiatrist in charge of her treatment.

Two years later, David received a letter from his mother saying, "Do you remember that girl—I think her name was Manuela—you used to moon over so much when you were in high school? I heard she was found dead from an overdose."

The night I met Lincoln

Hitchhiking as a newly arrived foreign student, I visited the Lincoln homeland: his log cabin birthplace in Kentucky and his home in Springfield, Illinois. For the climax of my pilgrimage, I had saved the Lincoln Memorial in Washington.

My ride let me off at midnight by the steps of the Memorial. As I approached it, all I could see was the enormous structure by the moonlight.

Suddenly the beam of a guard's flashlight fell upon me. "We're closed now," he said, approaching me. He was a tall African-American in a neat uniform.

We chatted and when he learned that I was a foreigner, he said, "There's a lot of talk in other lands about the problem with blacks here in the United States -about discrimination and prejudice. And yet, there's no single minority group anywhere that has made as much progress as we have. I'm about to enter law school."

"I will tell my friends abroad what you've just said." I bade him good-bye, picked up my suitcase, and was about to descend the steps when he called:

"Stay here while I put on the lights. Look up, boy—you're gonna have the treat of your life!"

I stood quietly, waiting.

The lights shone first on Lincoln's head, casting his shadow on the wall and leaving the rest of the chamber in a strange twilight; and then the brighter lights fell upon him.

Long I stood there awed by all the serene majesty of the man who now sat in stony silence but whose voice and deeds had guided his nation. I wondered about the people who had made such a nation possible. In the spell of Lincoln's presence, the spirit of their million voices answered, ringing out the wondrous words of liberty!

Cousins

I am looking at this photograph taken in Holland long ago. Here we are, four small cousins: Hánzi and Pali and Ernö and me tugging at my mother's skirt on a clear day at the Scheveningen beach before the war. Grandpa Jakob was happy taking the picture.

He had taken us to a Gypsy's tent on the promenade near the sand to have our fortunes told. A fat lady decorated from head to foot, trinkets and veils dangling all over her, came through a yellow curtain and sat on a big green pillow before the astonished eyes of us children, who looked at her amazed. After she made herself comfortable, she gazed at us, one after the other and asked to see the palms of our hands.

The Gypsy predicted a long life when Ernö and I dared to put our hands in hers. But her eyes froze and her words stumbled when Hánzi and Pali showed theirs.

"The lifelines go into….nothing," she whispered. Then she tried to force a better destiny on them by saying more cheerfully, "If you take good care you'll also live long and happy lives."

Out again on the boardwalk, Grandpa Jakob, intent on repairing the Gypsy's words, put on his skullcap and said a prayer.

"I don't need to look at my grandchildren's palms to know their fortunes," he said later, determined to change the fortunes of the two boys whose lifelines were cut off.

"No spell will be cast upon your lives: the oldest of you, Hánzi, will be a great actor. I've seen you clown around like nobody can! And you, Pali -because of your loving nature- are destined to save the lives of the sick, maybe discover the cure for a bad disease. Ernö: you, who are so good at reciting the Torah, will surely become a famous attorney defending the rights of the poor. And you, Bandikám, youngest of my grandchildren, whom I taught to read, have a writer -perhaps even a poet- inside you."

Jakob smiled when, for a reassuring moment, a panoramic view of his own existence merging into the lives of his grandchildren and beyond, unfolded before him toward a wholesome future. "Now, let me take your picture so we'll have proof of this day," he said as we heard the camera click.

Which one of the two fortunetellers of that balmy afternoon on Scheveningen had seen more of the youngsters's fate was to remain a mystery. There are those who say that modern science has not caught up with the occult arts of certain Gypsies nor the cabalistic notions handed down from antiquity as revelations to old Jews -both proclaiming that not a single blade of grass rises from the Earth unblessed by the loving hand of a divine being. And there are those who believe that our fate is as random as the burning of those faded blades of grass on the mountain slope when the jagged edge of lightning strikes haphazardly upon the Earth before the great storm is unleashed.

No one bothered to keep score, but in the blinking of an eye, just a few years after the happy outing where their destinies were foretold, Hánzi and Pali, lovely innocent youths, were forced to enter a gray sealed chamber leading nowhere (like the lifelines in their palms) in a remote village in southern Poland called Oswiecim— known also with a shudder of terror as Auschwitz—by the uniformed supermen guards in the midst of a great sea of moans around them and were gassed and turned into smoke with the latest product of Germany's marvelous technological achievement, a lethal substance called Zyklon B, until death set them free.

Their last consolation, while they took deep breaths, was to die together as the good friends they had always been.

Grandpa Jakob closed his eyes peacefully in bed before the invaders who dropped from the sky had a chance to take him away and never opened them again.

My mother died an old and wise woman with her many memories.

Ernö was a respected attorney in Holland until he died at the age of 79, no longer able to recognize his loving wife and family, not knowing his own name.

And I think about my little cousins from time to time.

In search of the past

David visited all the places where his ancestors had lived in the Danube basin. He first went to the town of Novi-Sad (known as Ujvidék when it belonged to Hungary) across the flat terrain of the border into Yugoslavia, where his uncle Mihály, whom he had never met -the one who had lost a leg during the First World War-, had settled with the nurse who attended him in the hospital.

For three days David inquired everywhere in town about his uncle but no one seemed to know anything about the man. The town had changed so much after the war, becoming a modern, charming and quiet little city. He knew that Mihály Rosenfeld had been among the more than a thousand Jews who were forced to jump into the icy waters of the Danube during the Winter of 1943 when the Nazis overwhelmed the town. But so many years had gone by and a new generation had arrived. No one recalled Mihály.

Walking along the Ulica Maxsima Gorkog avenue, a very old blind man stood on a corner with a weighing scale. David weighed himself and gave the man a few dinars. The man tipped his cap and clutched the bills with a broad smile on his face. But never in all his experience did David ever see a face turn from such an open smile into an expression of utter pain as the moment when he asked the blind man if he knew anything about Mihály Rosenfeld.

The old man began to shake while he said in Hungarian, "I lost my whole family in the same massacre where he died. My wife and three children. But I escaped thanks to the help of a German Catholic family who kept me hidden in their home. There were many good Germans. I've thought about it every day since the morning it happened. Yes, I knew Mihály well. He was my friend. Come with me and I'll show you something."

The blind man picked up his little weighing scale and placed under his arm a small sign he had for display. He held on to David. Together they walked toward the river, toward the spot on the shore where the Jews had been forced to jump into the Danube. Those killed were memorialized by a striking monument that stood next to the river, a bronze portrayal of the victims, a tall couple, naked, clutching each other, panic in their eyes, with a child clinging to them and a baby in the woman's arms, looking toward the river and beyond, as though they knew their time to die had come.

It all seemed so peaceful now. By the time they reached the monument, the man was panting, awash in tears. David was afraid he'd faint. "Let's sit down here first and rest a while," he said to the man. "I'll bring you a refreshment." But the man was adamant in his refusal. "No, no refreshment now," he said. "I want to show you. Come here with me to the foot of the statue." He oriented himself by touching the bronze child of the monument and positioning his own face to feel for the sunshine. "I'll show you the exact place," he went on, taking a few steps toward the river. "Right here," he pointed with his red cane, "there was ice on the river. It was the last week of January. They opened holes in the ice, and for three days brought hundreds of Yugoslavs and all the Jews of the town—most of them Hungarians—to the edge of the water. The Nazis brought Mihály shortly after dawn of the third day. His wife had been dead a few years and they had no children. He came fully dressed in his old uniform, a relic of the Hungarian Army, and he wore proudly on his chest all the commendations, medals and ribbons he'd received for fighting for our country. He was a real war hero, wounded at the Serbian front. He came on his crutches and stood up with his head held high. One of the officers made fun of him, ripped one of the medals off his chest accusing him of having stolen them and tossed it into the Danube, but Mihály didn't even flinch, just stood firmly, looking up."

The blind man stopped to catch his breath, took a dirty rag out of a pocket and wiped the sweat on his face and forehead before he went on: "They ordered him to jump in the hole they had opened by shelling the ice. Without saying a word, Mihály dropped his crutches to one side, saying with contempt, 'Give those to someone who needs them,' and jumped into the hole, the bravest man I ever saw, his death a slap in the face of his executioners. We loved our old country—dear Hungary—so much more than our Hungarian tormentors did. They'll never know how much. I was there a few yards behind him in the line of victims, waiting for my turn. I didn't mind dying. My whole family was gone. So many people came to watch the decorated soldier being killed by other soldiers that a crowd formed and in the confusion I moved up the bank and a German friend helped me get away and hide."

Now the ice was gone. It was warm. David liked Novi-Sad, the kind of town he might have chosen to spend part of his life. He stayed until the next morning when he got up at dawn and slowly walked toward the monument, touched for a lingering moment the head of the young boy and continued in the direction indicated by the old man the previous day, the same path his uncle Mihály had taken. He stood there, waiting by the edge of the water, looking at the evanescent whiteness of the fluffy clouds as they moved like ships in their journey toward the horizon. But nothing happened. Peace seemed eternal and soothing.

Far away in the sky, a flock of geese circled in perfect formation below the clouds, crying out in unison. All was calm and the smooth waters of the Danube moved on quietly downstream toward Romania. David was alone by the edge of the river on this warm morning under the blue sky. As he bent down, in search of Mihály Rosenfeld, trying in vain to tenderly reach across the decades back into the time of death, a few drops fell on his extended arm. But it wasn't raining.

"We're also human beings"

David was surprised by the welcome reception he received in the remote village of Gacsály in the southwest corner of Hungary, near the border with Ukraine and Romania, where the first Rosenfeld—his great-great grandfather, David ben Jakab, had settled with his family. When the villagers—mostly peasants—heard he was asking about his ancestors, they came to talk to him. They offered him wine and *palinka*, a drink stronger than brandy. A few of them invited him to stay in their homes since there were no tourist accommodations in the village. They showed him to the house where one of his grand-uncles had lived, known as the house of the stork's nest because on its thatched roof the storks had built an enormous nest where each Spring they hatched their eggs.

David was informed that twenty families of Jews had lived in Gacsály at the time of their deportation to the north. "They were taken to Auschwitz and we never heard from them again," the oldest one said, while the others stood silently shaking their heads. "The train came slowly from Transylvania, picking up Jews in the villages, filling up the cattle cars. By the time it arrived in Gacsály the cars were full, but they crammed them in and went on to Auschwitz. I'll never forget the wailing of the people inside the cattle cars, pleading for a little water and food."

An old peasant riding a dilapidated bicycle approached the group surrounding David in the middle of the street. When the man overheard the conversation, he said: "I knew two of the Rosenfeld brothers. We went to elementary school together. Mózes, who died in '25 and József. They were the tavern keepers. My name is Puskás Endre and I'm 75 years old. Nothing ever hurt me more than to see our own fellow townspeople jailed and deported."

Another man, dressed in a suit, introduced himself to David quite formally, saying, "I am Kallai Ference and I'd like to invite you to my house for a meal." He was older than the others and had known Sarah Rosenfeld, David's great-aunt. "She married her first cousin, András Roth," he said. "Their son, Jakob Roth, was my age. We were only 15 at that time, when the soldiers deported him and his whole family. I was sick with rage, but there was nothing we could do. The tyrants had the guns and all of us had to shut up. The Statárium Law adopted late in 1943 gave them the right to kill anyone for any offense. This happened in March of '44, just a year before the war ended."

The peasants showed David where the Roth family had lived, right in the center of the village on Petöfi Sándor Street. "Look," Ferenc said, pointing across the street from the house where the Roths had lived, "right there, in that lot which has remained empty all these years, was the place where all the Jews of this region were held for two days while they waited for the train from Romania that was packed with Jews from all the villages of Transylvania on its way north. The soldiers went to the homes of the Jews, rounded them up throughout the countryside, including the ones in Csenger—the town next to Gacsály—about 200 in all, and brought them to this little place, held them behind that fence."

It was a grassy lot of about 3000 square meters with a well in the center, located between the Reformed Lutheran Church and the local high school.

In the evening, David went to the home where his distant relatives had lived, occupied now by Istvánné Varga, who had offered to put him up when she learned who he was.

"I was a grown woman when the Jews of Gacsály were deported," she said. "I saw them at the gate across the street when they were brought there, one by one, dragged out of their homes. Half the town congregated around the gate and on the other sides of the lot that served as detention camp, afraid to be seen crying. They were our neighbors and friends. I remember how the townsfolk brought them food, though the soldiers forbade it. Still, some of them turned their heads the other way and allowed the prisoners to be fed."

That evening, after scarcely eating the meal Mrs. Varga prepared, David walked the two blocks to the only tavern in town, the same one that was once owned by his grand-uncles. Each peasant insisted on making his special speech, glass in hand, to honor the Rosenfelds. "Here's to your grand-uncle Mózes," one of them said, downing a glass of aged

Tokay wine, the 7 *putonos* kind that leaves a pleasantly sweet and warm feeling from the lips clear into the pit of the stomach.

In that small tavern that had belonged to his ancestors, David drank to their memory, trying to imagine the kind of life they had. Late at night, his head swirling, he took the walk back to Mrs. Varga's place, the old home of Armin Roth, who was chased out of his bed and dragged barely a few feet away into the strange land just across the familiar street he had walked on every day of his life, all his possessions confiscated in a moment. His wife, Vilma Rosenfeld, who was also his first cousin, was by his side as well as their grown child András with his wife Sarah and their son Jakob, going on 16. Jenö Rosenfeld and Etelka—so old she could hardly walk—were brought from the house of the stork. Distant cousins and relatives, Armin's parents, friends and all the Jews they had known in the county for years, arrived during two days and nights of terror.

David, very unsteady on his feet, slowly made his way over the dusty road.

For a while he stood swaying in the middle of the street. By his right was Armin's old home, the place where the kindly old widow was putting him up for the night to sleep in the comfort of his grand-uncle's bedroom, with the pillows and blanket stuffed with goose feathers, where his relatives had lived peacefully for so many years; on his left, by the church with the tall spire was the open iron gate and the dark, grassy enclave that had served as detention camp. David looked from right to left, from the inviting little house with the well-kept garden to the barren darkness of the empty lot.

Far down the street in front of him, beyond the two storied high school building, a bare light bulb fluttered weakly in the desolate night. He walked into the darkness and grabbing the iron fence he swung it around. It squeaked until it shut behind him. Not a single star could be seen in the night. Only a few years, he thought as he heard the gate lock, separated him from the events that had taken place there, only a few years, a blinking of the eyes. Thirsty, he placed his hand between the iron bars in the universal gesture of all mendicants and extended his arms trying to reach out as far as possible. "Water, please, water."

"Only a question of a little time and the soldiers would be here carrying me away with my family." He sat there in the dark and could almost see the soldiers's arrogant faces, hear their insulting commands, witness their acts of brutality while they "carried out orders." He shook his head and closed his eyes, trying to conjure up the faces of people he loved, relatives whom he had never seen and quietly began to sob.

He was told by the townspeople the names of some of the Gacsály Jews who had been held in that place, in that same darkness, over half a century before: beside the Rosenfelds and Roths they mentioned the Stern, the Schwartz, the Weiss, the Berger, and the Meyer families. David pondered long into the night about his own life, how he and his parents had survived. Hadn't he discovered during the long introspections of his psychoanalysis that he had disliked having a name that had been imposed forcefully by the conquerors on his ancestors? Hadn't he resented when he was a child in South America being a Jew when all his friends were not? Wasn't the child in him afraid of being a Jew? "Dr. Rosenfeld, Dr. Rosenfeld, " he mumbled, "it's time for you to go to the gas chamber." Sitting against the wall of the well in the middle of the lot he finally fell asleep.

In the morning he asked Mrs. Varga for directions to the Jewish cemetery. She frowned. "The old one was abandoned when they left," she said. "It might still be there, up this street toward the railroad station outside of town."

Tall grass concealed the little cemetery, but David found it. It was full of debris, a dumping place for trash, some of the tombstones overturned, some broken. It was difficult to walk with so much waste and wild growth. He knew this was the same cemetery his aunt Gizi, the foreseer of persecutions, had found vandalized in her youth. He didn't mind all the weeds that were growing among the graves, but resented the trash and -as she had done so long ago- set out to move it away. He brushed away some of the leaves from a cracked tombstone that lay on its side, pulling the dirt and moss from the faded Hebrew letters so he might read the inscription, hoping to find his namesake David ben Jakab's resting place, but the letters were undecipherable. None of the names on the other tombstones were legible either. Those who were interred there had merged into complete anonymity. But he knew his ancestors were buried there and touched each of the overturned gravestones with tenderness.

As he was finishing his task, a few peasants came to see what he was doing and expressed regret for the condition of the place, but he ignored them and completed his chore in silence. He wanted to get out of Gacsály and never come back. He wanted to leave as soon as possible but an urge to get some flowers and brighten up the dilapidated and vandalized cemetery, made him return to the center of the village where he had seen a cheerful garden. He knocked at a door and asked the woman who came out whether he could have a few flowers to take to the Jewish cemetery. She seemed surprised. "I didn't even know there was a Jewish cemetery in Gacsály anymore," she said.

"What there's left of it," David said a bit sullenly. "It's vandalized, full of debris. All the tombstones are overturned, smashed, with pieces taken away. I cleaned some of it."

"I am so sorry," she said. She handed him a large bouquet of beautiful flowers she cut for him and refused to accept any money. "No, thank you," she said. "After all, we're also human beings."

"I'd like to remember you by your name," he told her.

"It's Kiss Gabor."

David went back to the cemetery, placed the flowers upon the tombstones—an act contrary to Jewish custom—and drove to the railroad station.

Hitler had announced that those who did not work preparing the meal in the kitchen would not be able to sit down at the banquet table, so Hungary joined him and got back the territories ceded to Romania after World War I. As soon as the ruling government of the Arrow Cross Party came to power in Hungary the Jews of Transylvania were handed over to the Third Reich in exchange for the recovered homeland. Most Hungarians—eager for a reunification—were glad: at worst, a well-worth sacrifice.

When David reached the station he took several photos of the tracks going toward their final destination in the north and of the building and its well kept garden. As he did so, the station master appeared and addressed him harshly, "What do you think you're doing, taking pictures at a border town railroad station? Don't you know it's forbidden? I'm going to confiscate your camera."

"This is the village where my ancestors lived and I came to say good-bye to them at the Jewish cemetery. This is the railroad station where they were placed on cattle cars and shipped off to Auschwitz so I took pictures of it and their village, their vandalized cemetery, that's all that's in the camera. You want that?"

The station master, imposing in his uniform, looked at David and shook his head: "What am I supposed to do with you now?" He threw up his arms. "Promise me you'll never show anyone the pictures you took of the railroad depot and I'll let you go."

David got back into his rented car and left. As he drove away he remembered the woman who gave him the flowers and wondered if the same words she had spoken—"After all, we're also human beings"—had been uttered as well long ago when the train journeyed to Poland with its cargo of terrorized humanity.

TROPICAL BLOOMS

Saint Weepy

She got off the bus that brought her through the desert from the interior, wearing a baseball cap, her blue jeans stuffed into high boots shining in the sweltering heat of the tropical sun, carrying her large suitcase. Her behavior indicated that she was well able to take care of herself. A pride that bordered on arrogance, defined her as a being completely competent to do whatever she pleased at any hour of the night or day, without asking anyone's permission or counsel, totally above the daily tribulations of common folks, beyond mundane little problems.

They warned her that the closest village was at least forty kilometers away toward the north, on the other side of a dense forest and treacherous swamps, but she insisted that she knew of a small hamlet by the sea in the region and that she would find it. The bus driver, a giant of a man full of tatoos, freckled and displaying a few golden front teeth, looked at her with covetous eyes, fully realizing how attractive she was, and yelled at her: "Take good care of yourself, Little Red Riding Hood, for a pack of wolves may come and eat you tonight!"

Instead of being intimidated, she pulled up her loose blouse that covered a thick leather belt where she carried a revolver and, placing a hand over its breech—half threatening to take it out—she answered: "In that case you'd better let the first six wolves know they'll have to eat a bullet first!"

Just before dark she found the path she was searching for. Long ago she had walked on it when her family brought her sailing on a yacht to the village on the bay. They had stayed there for weeks, exploring the surrounding area. In the intervening years the brush had grown and the path was difficult to find.

The place she was looking for was further away than she remembered but she wasn't frightened when darkness fell and she had to stop for the night. She took out a mantilla from her suitcase and went to sleep by the side of the path with her revolver out of its holster safely tucked under her arm, next to her bosom. No one bothered her. When dawn awoke her, she continued walking until she reached the sea. She recognized the bay and knew that by continuing to walk toward the west on its shore she would find the hamlet.

When she arrived no one recognized her. The place had grown since she last saw it. Now, there was a row of huts on the open beach and a few sturdier adobe houses with tile roofs and large patios full of banana and coconut trees. She remembered the roving monkeys near the dwellings and smiled. They were still there playing at the top of the palm trees, looking for coconuts, waiting for hand-outs from the villagers. It was a memory she had treasured.

When she last visited, the children her age had come to the side of the yacht in their canoes gawking at her blonde hair and white skin. And when she came to shore they surrounded her, eager to touch her long hair, saying it was corn silk, wanting to touch it while she, in turn, took delight in rubbing her hands against their kinky, short, black hair, matted and rough. Now, those same children were young men and women like herself and they marvelled at her even more. For she was most unusual.

Not only did her beauty and the clothes she wore set her apart from others, but also her deportment, especially the way she looked straight into the eyes of those near her, without hesitations, so assured of herself, so immediate with her questions and answers, that it made everyone self conscious in her presence, especially the men.

Long ago she had rejected the submissive ways taught by strict nuns at the religious school where her affluent family interned her to finish her high school studies. After she graduated, they had hired teachers of etiquette and poise, in the fashion of their Spanish ancestors. Having won the first prize at a pageant in her province, she was sent as its most successful ambassador to the National Beauty Contest at the country's main sea port, whose finalist was chosen to be sent in turn to the Miss Universe contest that usually took place in one of the great metropolitan centers beyond the sea.

One of the judges, a majority stockholder of the commercial enterprize sponsoring the event, had approached her with a well studied assault of flattery during a festive occasion before the final event and tried to seduce her.

"Darling," he whispered to her when no one could see them. "I guarantee that at the finals the day after tomorrow, the other judges —all of them close friends of mine—will follow my recommendations …..my instructions, that is."

"Oh, I hope they'll like me," she answered.

"That depends entirely on you," he said, his mellifluous voice oozing, while he pointed at a small island on the horizon. "Let me give you a special tour of my island. It's deserted. No one will ever know we were there. It'll be our special pleasure and secret."

Discerning his intentions, she looked at him with a glacial disdain that left him flat. But two days later she lost the contest, though she received the consolation prize. The title she had longed for, the one with which she had hoped to represent her nation in the forthcoming international competitions, had slipped through her fingers. But she didn't feel dishonored and didn't regret for a moment her rejecting the invitation to spend the night with the judge on his island. When it was all over, when she was by herself staring in the mirror, not a tear was formed in her eyes. Yet, years later, the day after she settled in the remote bay after the long bus ride through the desert, the natives began to call her "Weepy." And it was the men who first gave her that nickname.

The village had less than thirty huts spread through the hillsides surrounding the bay. Some of the humble dwellings were built on posts by the edge of the sea, so close to the waves that when the tides came, they were licked by the foam.

It was noon when she arrived at the hamlet. She walked over to the first person she saw and inquired about empty lots that might be for sale. She was told that it was only necessary to build on a piece of land to claim ownership. After asking a few questions, and having inspected the surrounding empty lots, she decided upon a fertile promontory thick with palm trees somewhat away from the rest of the huts. It was a small peninsula from where the enormous extension of the bay could be seen on one side with its offshore oil derricks barely visible in the misty distance and a view without obstacles of the magnificent open sea on the other side.

She was the most beautiful woman ever seen in the region. The men who came to work for her didn't even dare to look at her eyes. They were black fishermen whose enslaved ancestors in Jamaica had escaped from their bondage and wandered across the Caribbean on their boats toward the mainland of the Latin American continent in search of land and freedom. For generations, most of them had not left the region. A few of them worked on the oil derricks. What they liked most was to fish and talk. They spoke a language nobody else could understand, except for a few fragments of their conversation. It was a blend of their ancestral African dialect, the English that the British had bestowed on Jamaica and the clipped Spanish spoken on the Caribbean where the ends of most words remained silent. Their needs were fulfilled if their stomachs didn't grumble from hunger at the end of each day. They fished in the bay and in the sea current that wrapped around the northern edge of the green continent four kilometers from shore and they talked half the night about every detail of life in the village. Some of them cultivated small vegetable gardens next to their huts and raised a few pigs and cows. But the staple food was fish and fruits. The earth and the sea gave them what they needed to survive. Anything beyond survival was a luxury.

When she offered them jobs they accepted without asking how much would she pay them. She seemed to have thought of everything: an ample house with a large dining room was to be built on the peninsular promontory between the sea and the bay, with a path toward the beach and a long boardwalk bordering the bay's shore where boats could dock on the translucent waters. The boardwalk and the dock would be sheltered from the onslaughts of the sea around the bend of the peninsula, protected from the harshness of the wind by the uninhabited rocky islands between the bay and the open sea, where the harsh waves would break into peaceful waters. On the other side of the bend, where the great ocean murmured endlessly as it stirred the white and fine sand, next to the palm trees bent toward the sun, she planned to build cabanas on the silky domain of the sand. She could visualize turning the place into a comfortable yet simple paradise. Without superfluous adornments, a rustic luxury would emerge that she knew well would attract the wealthy from the cities, those who navigated on the waters of the bay on their yachts, the same way her own family had done when she was a child.

Even though it didn't bother her to sleep outdoors, unprotected from the elements, she ordered the men to build her bedroom before doing anything else. At the end of the first day of labors, by the time the sun bowed toward the colossal vault of the night's oncoming firmament, they had already cut into the luxuriant thicket by the edge of the forest where they would build the house and the cabanas. On the spot she designated for her dormitory, where the rhythmical roar of the waves could be heard as they crashed against the sand and the rocks, they placed a large mound of thin firewood that bent under pressure but was difficult to break. It was the wiry kind of wood called *matarratones* (mice killers) that was very common in the region. They covered the extensive mound with a large quantity of banana leaves in thick layers. The wood below with the leaves on top was like an enormous spring mattress.

She helped in their chores, glancing at them at times, studying the merits of each of the workers.

Years later she would remember that first night she spent in this comfortable nest made by the men of the village. For such a long time— ever since she had failed to win the beauty contest—she had conjured up in her dreams that hamlet, its isolation and the asylum it offered. For the first time in her life she felt safe, protected from the falsehood of a world that had taken advantage of her, rejecting her if she didn't comply with its demands, its urgent and constant bartering always at her expense. It was the world she had rejected after her father put her out on the streets for having lost her virginity a few months after the beauty contest, when she was no longer able to say no to her own growing needs. Had it not been for an aunt who tried to be an intermediary with her parents, she would have been completely at the mercy of those who subjugated her and of her own passions. Having tasted the forbidden fruit, no other pleasure could take its place for her. Money was given to her through the aunt so she could establish herself wherever she wanted, provided it was not in the capital city where all her relatives had their homes and businesses.

For a few years she lived alone in several cities, an assortment of men following her everywhere with only one wish. And she allowed them to take from her what they wanted because she enjoyed the act in itself, though she hated the hypocrisy of the men. She knew that what they yearned for had nothing to do with sharing their erotic joy, much less any noble or tender sentiment, but to subject her to their will, turn her into a vassal, oppress her, exploit her. Still, on each occasion, as she gave herself over, unable to resist the desire for the pleasure, she thought of that green oasis next to the vast desert, by the small forest bordering on the sea, sprinkled by its waves, promising peace. Wherever she went, judges, army brass, police chiefs, priests, physicians, industrialists, the town's wealthiest and most powerful, sooner or later, uttered to her the proposition that she lacked the will to turn down. No one could protect her against her own lust.

At the age of twenty-five she tried to find asylum in one of the smaller cities, where she hoped the reputation that began to follow her would cease but, shortly after her arrival, busy tongues of the town spread a rumor there as well and the whisperings began to speak again of her being a whore who resisted at first but soon succumbed, unable to exist without a virile member to satisfy her craving. Soon after, she purchased a gun and followed through with the plans she had forged to go back to the hamlet, knowing she would have to travel through the dangerous desert in her search for the village of blacks in the bay of her fondest memories. She promised to herself never to yield to either the rich or the whites, because they were the ones who had tormented her, vowing that she would choose her lovers from that moment on.

After the natives built the nest for her and brought her fish and fruits, they were about to return to their huts, when she said to them: "One of you can stay with me tonight because I don't like to sleep alone."

She nearly closed her eyes, all the better to watch their reaction in secret through the veil by her long eyelashes.

The eight workers stood gaping, stunned by her words. None of them moved. No one volunteered.

"Well, let's see," she went on. "I'm going to pick up eight little sticks. I will hide them in my hand so you will only see their ends. Each one of you can pick a stick and the one who will show me the longest, can sleep with me. If you wish, tomorrow we'll have another raffle."

Having discovered that beauty can be found anywhere, she looked at one of the men who was the least handsome among the workers. In her eyes, he was strong and had an evanescent, almost shy smile and a friendly sparkle in his dark eyes that attracted her, even though a cruel accident had practically deprived him of the use of one of his legs, which he dragged around in an awkward and self-conscious way.

Spying him, she smiled and told herself, *El hombre es como el oso: mientras más feo, más hermoso* (Man is like a bear: the uglier, the prettier.)

But the first night she was won by a young man who bragged about having crossed the bay swimming all the way to the oil derricks barely visible on the horizon. She took out a perfumed piece of soap from her suitcase and proposed taking a bath together on the beach under the last rays of the sun. When the young man began to shed his clothes, she refrained him and, swallowing, she said: "Wait for my help."

He, surprised and a little frightened, allowed her to peel off the scant clothes he had worn during the day, feeling that every part of his body surged and became uncontrollably rigid the moment she touched him. With an eagerness unmanifested earlier in the day, even during the most enthusiastic moments of selecting the plot of land where her home would be constructed, she unbuttoned his clothes. Seeing him naked, she enjoyed the sight of the prodigy of manhood her avid eyes found.

"I congratulate you," she said to him. "You pack a most goodly portion of meat there, worthy of a Greek god."

Later, much later, when the moon had reached its zenith and the sky found itself replete with scintillating stars in the immensity of space, when she and he were only two embraced shadows devouring each other like two jungle beasts in heat, when at the culminating moment both lost their breaths and felt emptied, as though suspended among undiscovered nebula in a world of their own, she wailed on and on from the joy she felt while he groaned above her. Tears flooded her and her prolonged sobs were clearly heard throughout the hamlet and the forest surrounding the bay. It was on the following day that the men of the village began to call her Weepy.

On the second day, the workers began to cut the wood to build the house and the cabanas, but instead of eight helpers fifteen came, some of them shy boys who looked at her out of the corner of their eyes with a sideward glance and an inexpressible hope. At the end of the day's work, the same ritual of the previous evening was undertaken. This time, one of the youngsters barely past fourteen years of age won the raffle. Very timid and without any previous experience in such matters, but extraordinarily eager, he allowed himself to be taught by her. And again, when the culminating moments of her pleasure arrived, she shed her tears of joy and in the last instant began the wailing that carried her cries above the waters of the bay.

Much work was accomplished on the third day because all the able bodied men and adolescent boys of the village came to help. After the arduous task, after the ritual of the little sticks was over, she spent the night upon her mice killers and the banana leaves, the spring mattress so lovingly provided for her, with the fellow they all called El Feo, which meant The Ugly One, the one she had spied and lusted after on her first evening in the village. That night, Weepy cried louder and longer than ever.

Months later, when they had finished building her house, the dock and the cabanas, all the males above thirteen years of age, including the old fishermen who fished from the shore and who approached her place at the hour of the raffle before sunset, had enjoyed her favors. She refused no one.

When she found out that they called her Weepy in the village, she didn't care. "Before, I never cried," she said. "Now my beautiful blacks make me cry with happiness every night. That's how I like it." But those who had paid close attention to her cries noticed a slight sorrowful accent mixed in with the passionate moans at times and wondering why, were surprised to hear her say: "I also weep because I know there's much suffering in this world."

In the beginning, she had very little to do with the women of the village. They smiled knowingly when they'd see her and a few of them, having heard the men's gossip about Weepy, resented her. But when she saved a little girl's life, risking her own, coming between the child and a venomous snake that was about to bite her, killing the menacing viper in the last instant with a well aimed bullet to its head before it leaped to deliver its lethal bite, the women of the village began to lose their early resentment.

She formed lasting relationships with everyone. If anyone became ill, Weepy would go to the hut of the sick person to help. She taught the women how to cook foreign dishes whose recipes she had learned from the french nuns. She assisted the midwife of the village. And if anyone needed something she had, it would appear at their doorstep before the day was over. She shared so gladly what she had that after a few years the women amended the nickname the men had given her and began to refer to her as Saint Weepy of the Peninsula. Even the men began to call her a saint just before she gave them their ultimate pleasure.

The first clients began to arrive during the summer vacation after the house and the cabanas were finished. Weepy raised an enormous purple flag at the very edge of her peninsula between the bay and the ocean with the word Inn written on it in big white letters that the sailors could see with their high powered binoculars from great distances. They'd approach in their yachts and circling near the shore, looking for a place to dock, they would discover the inviting moorage behind the rocks where the bay began and where they glided silently in the peaceful waters. Feeling protected from the harshness of the sea in the quiet cove where it was easy to dock, they were enthralled at the swaying palm trees that emerged like eager dancers on the pristine beach.

The inn acquired fame throughout the coast. And Weepy began to make money. But instead of keeping it to herself, she shared it. Whatever was needed by the villagers she got for them. She had a small clinic built where the medical needs of the villagers were met, hiring a nurse and a physician who came to the hamlet once a week. A soccer field followed and her next project was a playground for the children, with slides and merry-go-rounds for the smaller ones.

Weepy installed a powerful motor on a large canoe and went to the distant city on the other side of the bay that still thrived the same way it had many years ago under the tropical sun, looking as though not a day had gone by since the pirates had held it hostage during the Spanish conquest. There, she was seen frequently buying what the villagers needed with the money she made at her inn. But she made sure she'd return before sundown to spend the otherwise interminable night with her lovers.

She'd personally wait on the owners of the luxurious yachts anchored in her moorage and, though she was friendly and often would be seen gaily laughing with them, she always kept her distance when it came to a more intimate relationship. She didn't trust them. Sometimes, she appeared to promise to fulfill the yearned dreams of one or another of her clients. It seemed that the more they wished to seduce her, the more they consumed in her inn, leaving greater amounts of money. But she wasn't interested in them. "I only love my blacks," she'd say.

The visitors, often powerful men with vast fortunes, watched her in the evenings while she played a strange game of sticks with fifteen or twenty half naked men and boys. There was such merriment among them, such a natural flow of feelings. None of the visitors ever knew what the game was about and when they asked, the natives smiled and giggled: "It's a game Saint Weepy taught us long ago."

Through the years, Weepy added new details to the rites of her raffle: instead of the longest stick, the *five* of greatest lengths would win the trophy.

Late into each night, by the light of a moon that spread its shimmering light over the waters of the bay, a woman's long cry could be heard intermittently for hours, sometimes becoming entangled with the outbursts of moans from a small group of men.

The sounds rolled in great waves beyond the cottages full of wealthy tourist, on to the bay where the luxurious yachts were anchored and then spread out to the glorious sea.

Mario's Hideaway

Doña María seemed to have no other desire in her life than guard her daughter Lucila's virginity. Although Lucila was in her mid-twenties and by the standards of Antioquian custom, bordering on spinsterhood, she was a beautiful woman with long, black hair and Moorish eyes, from a lineage that stemmed from ancient Granada.

It was rumored that the reason so many of the students at the all-male Escuela de Minas (School of Mines), located across the street where Lucila lived, flunked out, was not because of the inordinate difficulty of the courses taught there. The young men just wore themselves out mooning in vain after Lucila and had no energy left for their studies. They came to court her by her window, where she was protected from their longing by an iron grill and by her mother, doña María, who sat behind her and made her presence known, coughing whenever passion would lead the ardent young men to daring acts, such as putting their hands across the grill to make the most elusive contact with Lucila's smooth skin, in that penumbra from where tormenting and exciting perfumes emanated.

No one knew what tests of frustration and endurance doña María fashioned for her beautiful daughter and those admirers who courted her for nearly two decades, but the years passed and she remained unmarried, chained as it were to her window until her charms waned and no one stopped to share with her any of the illusions of youth. Her most consistent suitor, don Mario, a handsome engineer, stood by her window for years, often with his umbrella under the torrential tropical rain, passing out pennies to the children of the neighborhood so they would play somewhere else and give him a few moments of privacy with his beloved. After many years of courting Lucila he gave up and moved to another city.

Several generations later, the house where the overpious mother shackled the burning passion between beautiful Lucila and Mario, was transformed into a small café where lovers held secret trysts. The name given to the establishment was Mario's Hideaway.

PRE-REVOLUTIONARY SCENES
IN LATIN AMERICA

The birth

Slowly, she began climbing the hill. No one noticed. Most of the women her age climbed the hill at least once a year; and now it was her turn, her first time. She planned to climb it many times in her life.

If only she could have finished the work before the pains made it impossible to continue. But the pains had been great and they had mounted in intensity as the day wore on. Now the sun was setting, shadows were lengthening and soon it would be dark. If she did not reach the lake in time, maybe something bad would happen.

She did not want anything bad to happen. Not her first time.

Here was the path up the hill. If she followed it the lake would be at the end, where one need not be afraid of evil because the moon was there, looking down. She would finish the work tomorrow.

Her feet dug into the dirt and she stopped a moment to bring some of it up with her toes. Bending down, she picked up the dirt and rubbed it on her abdomen with her hand, under her skirt. This was good dirt. Dirt that made things grow.

Yes, tomorrow she would finish the roof. She had threaded it already with corn silk, thickened it with banana leaves and palms, made it strong by soaking all of it in the river and letting it dry under the sun, poured grease over it so the rain would not drip into the hut. All she had to do was tie it firmly to the ditch reed so the wind would not blow it down. She felt strong and free when thinking about the wind.

She looked back and saw the shadows closing in on her. She continued walking and after a while she realized it was dark and she saw little spots of light as they touched the ground and the leaves in the trees, as they hid behind the grass.

Then she began to feel the pains again, more intensely than ever. But her face was still, and she did not complain. She lifted her skirt and rubbing more dirt on her abdomen she looked down and said:

"Wait. Yet it is not the time."

And she thought she must hurry, for her load was impatient.

Now she began moving faster with her legs spread apart, holding her breath, sweating, tensing the muscles of her abdomen, biting into her lips until she felt blood run down her chin and something warmer run down the inside of her legs.

It was dark when she reached the top of the hill where she sat down beside the lake but it was light above, where the moon had come to meet her.

She rested a while, and when she could breathe more easily she reached for a few banana leaves and placed them on the humid ground, then found two large stones. Holding one stone in each hand she crouched on the banana leaves, facing the moon and spreading her legs. And then she looked into the face of the moon, thrusting her pelvis forward and squeezing the two stones into the earth she cried in the night:

"Now is the time of the coming! Come! Come! Come!"

But the child would not come and she saw the moon looking down, eternal frozen wanderer of the purple space among the stars, until it was so pale she knew the dawn must arrive.

She saw the formless clouds were shaped by the winds, transformed into gigantic men that filled the whole sky, marching across the firmament, moving worlds, leaping over the flaming horizon while at last she gave birth.

Between the night and the dawn she heard her babe cry, and making a last effort, she pressed her hands against her abdomen where the good dirt lay so the blood there would flow freely into the new life. This was good blood, blood that made things grow. Then she rubbed the cord that held their lives together with the two stones. And when the cord was broken and they were one no more, she felt relieved of her burden.

She examined the babe, touching it eagerly with her fingertips and felt the wild beating of her own heart, a beating that was now faster than ever before in her life. When she found that the child was a man, she smiled and looked up with tenderness at the pale moon.

Now she took the babe in her arms and walked into the waters of the lake, washing him well so the moon would admire him. She thought of the pride she would feel tying the roof onto the sticks of the hut with her babe on her back, with all the villagers gathered around, watching her, knowing that her first one was a man.

This was the beginning of a new day.

The conquest

Mist slowly rises when the early sun moves above the cordillera. Stand on one of the hills watching any of the rivers rush through the canyons until you lose sight of it in the immense jungles beyond, moving among the green vaults toward the sea, and if here is the place you were born, if on this part of earth you spent your youth, if your ancestors are buried by these hillsides, you will know with certainty that this land belongs to you.

You will see with the passage of time and the increasing warmth of the day the mist vanish and the vast fields clear, exhibiting their limitless beauty.

Toward the south, mountains leap out of the sea against the hostile Western winds. The mountains begin where the earth is cold, dark and deserted. At times, the hills surrender and fall against the sea forming cliffs and islands, but soon they rebel against the turbulent waters that do not let them surge, and moving into the arms of the continent they climb toward the sky, forming the most sovereign heights of the world. Should you go eastward, you will first see the savage pampas which extend into infinity.

If you walk toward the north, you will see impenetrable jungles, enmeshed with profound rivers. Later, much further North and West, by the warm oceans, by the beaches of soft sands where the horizons open, you will feel the sensuousness of the tropics in the fertile hillsides and in the valleys of incomparable beauty where you will be embraced by your country's mountains.

Even as a stranger who has never seen this place, you will know with certainty that the road to a lovelier homeland does not exist; and if that earth were to sneak into your blood, you'd know you love her because the promise she makes is that of freedom.

But if you had lived here for a thousand years and could no longer tell your hand from the earth it clutches; if you had scraped the fertile ground with your daily sweat; if in your idolatry you had molded its clay to worship it; if your mother had rubbed it into your entrails even before your birth; and yet, neither your work, nor your love, nor your death could make the land yours, then not even sky, nor time, nor the gods, or the hundred loathsome plagues and wars whose torments and pestilence have been your daily companions, or the infernal fire of the conqueror's tyrannical descendants with their ultramodern weapons of steel, could prevent you from rising one day with your clenched fists scraping the skies to claim what is yours and what you are. And you'd know as surely as you sense when you look out from the top of the cordillera that there is no greater beauty than what you see, that no matter how long it will take, the day will arrive when you will surely leap enraged like the mountain's condor to rip out the eyes of your oppressors, or when you will come close to them at the least expected hour as it was taught to you by the viper that crawls through your deserts, to poison the blood of your tormentors, to recover the land that was stolen from your ancestors. For the earth belongs to those who touch it lovingly with their breath and their daily sweat.

You will stand there on the top of the hill knowing that this feeling of the earth is the only one that gave you strength even on the implacable dawn when our captors appeared five hundred years ago wrapped in the mist of the river; when we first heard the thundering noise of the hooves of their mighty horses suddenly razing our placid valley, bearing those impudent riders with armor and lance, with their terrible spewing fire, with their shield and their cross; those creatures who turned out to be men like us but who, upon first seeing them, could not be differentiated from the beasts they mounted because we had never seen a man on a horse before; those bearded beings who roared in a strange language, whose skin was like the river's foam and who craved for gold the way we crave for water when on our long journey we thirst through the dusty deserts far away, the way we crave for salt when the meat of the hunt is about to be consumed, and as we will always crave for freedom.

Before the invaders arrived in our village, we gathered the gold and the treasures of our beloved gods and carried them to the top of the hill where we were born for generations, where a lake awaited us, where one need not be afraid of evil because two gods would be there to protect us, one through the lonely night while the other watches us throughout the long day.

Those of us who climbed to the top of the mountain that day numbered over one thousand, counting the women and children. The old ones, the infants and the sick remained in the village. Silently, we cast all the possessions coveted by the white warrior into the deepest part of the lake. The gold and the engraved images studded with precious stones, sacred to us, sank rapidly in the deep and inaccessible shadow of the lake's bottom.

The sonorous echoes of the beasts were heard through the mountains. And then he appeared, wrapped in death's fury, scourging the valley with the frenzied gallop of his wild steed, he and his monstrous cavalcade, the ancient blasphemy of fierce conquerors on their livid lips and the bristling, crazed stampede suddenly exploded into a satanic thunderclap, leaving behind nothing but a trail of blood and ashes.

The following morning the huts stood like smoking torches on the immense, inflamed scar of the valley, crepitating toward the sky's throbbing sun.

Neither the gold nor the gods's images were found; only a few scraps among the abandoned ruins in the rush of the exodus. The invaders carefully searched each hut before setting it on fire and, not finding anything they valued, their fury mounted until at the noon of the second day they finally tore out a confession from one of the bleeding moribund tongues they had tortured without compassion.

The conquerors marched up the hill in file, desecrating our holy ground for the first time, in search of the villagers and elusive gold, certain of finding both at the summit by the lake. But when they eagerly tumbled upon the top of the hill, a macabre feast of death confronted them suddenly, and a suffocating stench of putrefaction overcame them, forcing them to retreat when they beheld the million fluttering feathers of countless vultures clapping a diabolical multitude of wings, death's own ovation to the cowardly victor, flitting savagely in sinister clouds from corpse to corpse with red, festive claws and beaks from which torn bits of entrails still lingered in their tugged, avid and gluttonous disputation. The scavengers gulped down the decaying flesh of the villagers who had hanged each other and themselves from the mango trees bordering the placid lake where many of the drowned women and children floated aimlessly. And those who swayed from the trees had made sure their backs would be turned toward the path where they knew the enemy must pass, to express their disdain and rage, so that even in death their pride would not expire, looking toward the lofty mountains at the moment of entering eternity and now with mute and frozen stares fixed upon the distant horizons of their homeland.

The gold was lost in the fathomless bottom of the lake. And the conquerors felt invaded by a numbness toward the villagers in their attempt to deny what they beheld. For a few moments only, their zeal for gold lay dormant, until beginning the descent to camp. Fleeing the nauseating stench and fearing a plague, they realized that a primitive people had preferred to die rather than live under their yoke. In the conquerors's retreat, the first they had suffered in all their campaigns in the New World—overwhelming each time the flimsy arrows with their fire spewing machines—they felt cheated, thwarted in the face of death, and their numbness turned into disbelief. They wondered indignantly how these barbarous heathens dared to show such obstinate contempt, such subtle derision, such utter rejection as to die with their backs turned toward such noble conquerors.

Night extinguished the light of day and a twilight curtain of eviscerated figures rested, closely watched by satiated sentinels. The vacuous eyes of the heavens, birds and the hanged villagers slowly closed upon the vivid image as the curtain of bodies and tree branches, barely oscillated by the soft, tepid breeze, became dense, undistinguishable, as bone rubbed against bone, leaf against leaf, flesh against flesh, feather against feather.

The dark, hushed, enormous wing of night slowly engulfed life and death, while the immortal dream of freedom rolled on among the stars as it had happened since the world began.

When dawn came, the soldiers attended Mass in the valley at the burial of two of the victors who had died -one from malaria and the other from an old wound- while the surviving villagers, mostly the elderly, the sick and lame, forlorn and burdened with the chains of a slavery they had never carried before, watched from afar in grave bewilderment, invaded by a recent fear which for them was unknown.

Ora pro nobis.

"Pray for us," the conquerors muttered.

As the prayers were mechanically repeated, the image of the endless rows of swarthy, half torn bodies hanging from the branches of the ghastly trees, and the spectacle of the floating bodies of women and children upon the waters remained with the conquerors. Years later, after they had returned to their own country, Mother Spain, the scene at the mountain lake was the image they recalled with greatest frequency and the memory which portrayed the indelible impression of this green continent of their conquest for the rest of their lives. Their senses dulled as they prayed, they knew that it was not possible to speak of pity or love toward their comrades in arms, these two men who came to die in this valley of the new world they were conquering in God's name and for the honor and glory of their king. Now, with the scene of horror still so fresh, they could think of nothing else. Kneeling in this savage land, it was strange how one could share with another soldier all the years of homeless hardship and fatigue, the exultation of a hundred battles, and yet feel so detached at the hour of his burial. Like an automaton, one could only repeat old words learned during childhood—*Dominus vobiscum*—and kneel again at the sound of the bell, smelling the strong odor of incense. And they looked away from the cross with the Christ stretched upon it, yet now and again surreptitiously peered toward the hill, toward the lake and the trees.

Nunc et in hora mortis nostre, amen.

Yes. Now and in the hour of our death.

The duel

Stand on top of the tall mountain, and if this is the place where you spent your youth, you will hear the soft murmur of the wind speak in the accents of freedom.

If you walk down the stony paths toward the river, you will know that man's inexorable steps have left deep furrows upon the splendid valley. Look around and you will see the many giant bridges under which the river moves forever, its strength already tamed, its power held; and watch the railroad along its shores taking man's ageless and agonizing toil toward the horizon and beyond. See the hundred factory chimneys point toward the sky. Tall buildings crowd the center of the valley, huddled against the cathedral, hunchbacked colossus whose somber, waxy arms hover mutely over the city, its extended fingers scraping the clouds.

Now you are far from the sea and the burning desert. You cannot hear the roaring turbulence of swollen waters nor the screaming sands, and neither ice nor snow will touch you.

Here, in this city you shall know poverty in your mother's arms. You shall look up at the sky and see her face, and she will sing a song in your ears, your own cradle song which you will repeat with the first words of your mouth, taught by the conquerors to your ancestors long ago. The song speaks of angels like yourself and of the life you will enjoy some day long after the scorpion will have made his nest within the socket of your eye. The song speaks of a home, celestial and free from care or rent or mortgage. It will not be made of manure or tin cans like your home on the hills of this world but of sweet, eternal love. Neither will it stand upon a piece of ground sold in small parcels on a twenty-year loan to those fortunate enough to escape the crowded tin slums, but in Heaven, where all things are possible and where you will see the face of God. And you will live happily ever after.

For ours will be the kingdom of heaven where we shall be comforted and filled. And we shall inherit the earth, obtain mercy, and shall sit by the right hand of God. We shall be called the children of God if we bury our wrath and forget the five hundred desolate years of our captivity. And we shall finally rest in the House of the Lord into all infinity if we keep our hearts pure while the cuckolds force our sisters to sell their bodies in the bright palaces of lust, if we hunger and thirst after righteousness while they keep us out of the universities and, above all, if we obey and submit.

But in the meantime, while the worm eagerly awaits our flesh, let the meekest and the hungriest among us beg for a piece of cardboard and a few yards of wire from the warehouses of the mighty; let him burrow and scrape into the dung heaps and the fortresses of garbage in the outskirts of the great industrial city and, with his wife and children, drag like crabs the scraps of discarded tin plates; fill their sacks with tin cans that only recently stored delicious foods they will never taste, and carry the glorious loot across the streets and fields and up the craggy peaks of the hills where the gallantry and generosity of the city fathers will allow him and a million others to carve out of the ground with his machete a small place to rest his head and build his own room of tin walls, tin roof, cardboard beds and newspaper mattresses at a reasonable price for the entire family.

He will build his room upon a high place overlooking the city, and if he can spare a few coins for bribery they will allow him to live near a creek where his pregnant wife will not have to work more than a few hours daily hauling water.

He will rise with the first sign of dawn and make his way down the teeming hillside among the other tin and cardboard rooms. And if he is to have good fortune, it will not be until late at night when he will return, exhausted and consumed from the work at the factory, where his powerful back will have carried enough bales of cotton to clothe him and his ancestors for five centuries.

But now let him drag his loot quickly through the prying streets, for greedy eyes haunt him and a man with a more bitter life than his, a larger family of starved children, a man even more battered by the whiplash than himself, more poisoned, already stalks and seeks him out as his own prey. With cunning eyes, panting with a furious heart, the gleaming of his unsheathed machete concealed under his ragged poncho, he waits for his victim around the deserted corner of a lonely street.

Fifty more years of sunshine stretch out before him, but he throws it all into the vortex and gambles everything against nothing.

Is it madness that hurls him on, suddenly screaming curses across the suffocating street against this unsuspecting adversary, or does he want to steal what the man has gathered?

A mighty roar that echoes down the empty streets reverberates, shrieking from the throat of the despoiler. His eyes bulge and the dark veins of his thick throat wildly throb with each stroke of his desperate heart. His left hand whirls the poncho, wrapping it around the taut muscles of his arm to shield his naked chest with rags, while his right hand firmly clutches the lethal weapon. Sensing the advantage of surprise he leaps confidently, pointing the hissing blade straight up as far as his arm can reach toward the sky for the added power the arm will need when it is brought down upon the dark, mute face of the victim, who turns and stares dumbly at the gaping mouth of his attacker only for as long as it takes the sun's reflection on the raised weapon to strike his eye and warn him of the descending danger.

And as men have always desperately attempted to interpose anything, no matter how flimsy or ephemeral, between themselves and their executioners, to gain, even in the gullet of disaster, another precious instant of prolonged existence, he placed one of the rusted pieces of tin—what was to become a part of his family's shelter in the turpitude of the hills—between himself and the shattering blade, brought down so mightily that the tin plate was impaled and the point of the blade trembled for an instant inside the prominent cheek of the victim, eliciting a torrent of blood and desperate, agonized screams from those for whom the wounded man had toiled: his wife who stood bewildered, unable to believe what was happening, feeling heavy with the weight of metal and pregnancy, and her small and startled children clinging to her faded skirt and dragging the sackfuls of tin cans, dissonantly clanging in the midst of the wailing street.

In spite of the vehement efforts of the attacker to maintain his initial advantage with a repeated avalanche of furious blows with the machete, the bleeding victim, now rolling in the dust, now leaping, now backing against a cement wall that served as a springboard to avoid the thousand eager flames brought near the flesh by the cutting edge, finally gained time through the momentum of his few furious steps to unsheathe in frantic desperation the redeeming, vengeful machete he carried by his waist. Letting his persecutor feel the impact of steel upon steel, he smiled savagely with a diabolical grin and spat blood on his face, screaming the ancient cry of anticipated victory which had always given the enemy pause, a moment to restore shrewdness and feel the sweet passage of time, to scheme the forthcoming mortal blows of the combat.

He began filling his lungs with air, avidly breathing like a man escaped from a whirlpool, laughing to cover up his panic, waving his machete with his right hand, his own poncho tightly wrapped around his left arm for shield, keeping his adversary at a distance, commanding his wife and children to get off the street, now cursing in a shrill, mocking voice to provoke impulsive attack, scratching the dirt with his toes and kicking dust toward the encircling enemy who, taken aback, was recovering and going through similar motions.

Now both are standing a few paces apart, scurrying sideways, waving the machetes in wide circles and taunting each other, rhythmically thrusting their pelvises forward while reaching down with all five fingers of the left hand and grabbing, tugging, shaking at each other their concealed and bulging sex organs under the thin drill pants, screaming curses back and forth, now moving their arms like the wings of fighting cocks and crowing wildly:

"*Hijuepuuuuuuta!* Son of a biiiiiiiitch!"

The wounded man's dribble of blood from his cheek was held back by a handful of dust he picked up in the street and pressed into the gash. His wife was on her knees, the loot of tin sheets and cardboards scattered on the street, with the children huddled against her. She raised her arms and wailed the prayer of the valley.

"Don't let them kill my man! Blessed God, don't take away my man!"

A few stray, cadaverous dogs, who chanced to hear the clamor and wailing in the street, barked in the distant corner and ensued a jaded trot toward the commotion, hoping for some kind and generous spirit to toss them a bite of food.

"There goes your mother whore with the rest of the scabby dogs!"

"Watch out bastard! I'm gonna kill you! Heee, heeee, heeee, heeee!"

His laughter was forced and frightened although it conveyed a confidence that continued to keep his assailant at a distance. The two men studied each other's movements carefully, feigning to leap forward, laughing, and then again retreating.

An enormous blood bubble formed above his mustache as he laughed, a viscous, pale-red, rotating bubble with bits of dust and mucous. It became larger until it reached down into his mouth and up toward his eyes. Then it burst as suddenly as it had formed, startling him and splattering a few speck of blood over one side of his face and into his glistening, black eye. He rubbed himself with the poncho, blinking. But in that instant he felt again the thousand suns burn his flesh and heard the strange wailing of his wife's voice and the barking of the dogs. The blade's point had penetrated through the shielded arm and he felt a dull ache in his elbow. His contender was already at a safe distance laughing and making teasing gestures like a rooster. When he noted that he already had two wounds bleeding profusely and perceived how the other man remained completely unhurt, he was infuriated and instead of retreating, he attacked savagely. He must cut into his enemy's flesh, feel its soft resistance and sense the impasse of the bone. He thought of killing him and tearing his body into bits with the machete.

The fury of incessantly screamed insults, shrill laughter, the clashing of blade against steel and cement, the terrified wailing of the prostrate woman and her children, and the mocking bark of the pack of dogs filled the street. A few of the shutters nearby opened and people began coming out of the houses and running down the street in their Sunday best. A great cry, raised by a hundred voices old and young, was added to the din and clamor of the battle, proclaiming the wild news with no intention of concealing the inward joy felt at announcing the great and free spectacle of two men engaged in a bitter struggle of life and death.

"*Pelea! Pelea!* Fight! Fight! Over here, with machetes! Yeeeeheeee! *Pelea!*"

In a few moments a great circle was formed, allowing a respectable distance between the fighters. And the more they screamed the more people arrived from adjacent neighborhoods until the street was filled. The sea of spectators flowing into the crowded street began to take positions on window ledges, balconies, tree branches, car tops and patio walls from where the observation and thorough enjoyment of the fight would be unimpaired.

So suddenly was the street invaded by the multitude that the two men had barely recovered from their last attempt to maul each other when they found themselves in a shifting, violent nightmare surrounded by these eager strangers. Though intent on following each other's movements they heard the shrill exclamations from the crowd:

"*Matálo, matálo!* Kill him! Cut him up! *Comételo vivo!* Eat him alive! Let's see who's the real macho!"

The grinning men looked at each other, their faces twitching, the wounded one trying to save strength by letting his attacker move in circles around him.

"Coooooooocureeeecoooo! Cooooooooocuuuuuuuriiiiicooooo!"

When they resumed their attacks against each other, a wild surge of approval came from the crowd. The excitement spread fast and the circle around the fighters tightened so dangerously close that when the machetes traced their sideways-sweeping, lethal orbits, the crowd pushed back and then forward again in a tempestuous wave under which the wife and children of the wounded man and some of the weaker spectators were trampled.

The ocean swelled and the overwhelming tide finally closed the circle completely, tossing into its current the wounded fighter and heaving him on top of his assailant at the very moment when his blade was aimed at his exposed dark skin above the wrapped poncho, aiding his thrust, adding a new fury to his impetus. Then he knew that his foe, this attacker who had assaulted him so treacherously during his peaceful task, would forever bear the indelible marks of his vengeance.

He screamed victorious, and the peculiar, instantaneous memory of a beggar with an amputated arm, huddled by the gates of the cathedral, crossed his vision as he saw the arm unhinge, limbering, as he saw a red fountain splash the dust, as he heard his enemy's wailing voice. But no sooner had his joy become known to him, no sooner had the vision been dipped in crimson and vanished, when he felt a tingling sensation on his own left wrist and sensed the tide of his blood pulling on his whole body as he tumbled and saw an emptiness, a red gap, his own stump, and unretrievably beyond his reach, his open hand, lonely in the multitude as it had always been, begging on the dust among the trampling feet.

The crowd ebbed, murmuring, and for an instant he thought he saw his wife crawling out of the circle of men surrounding him, crowding toward the resting hand that still bled as though it had a life of its own. He never knew whether he had dreamed it or if it actually had happened to him in the spring of his childhood in the hills's slums, but it seemed to him that long ago he heard a woman, perhaps his own mother, pray in gratitude to God for a pound of fresh meat that had been given to them, and he remembered how his mother's tears had fallen on the meat and she had kissed it, sobbing. It all seemed so confusing and strange now because he thought he saw her again and heard her praying, sobbing as she had done so many years ago, kissing that piece of bloody meat that inexplicably had the shape of his own hand, rocking it against her breast like a baby and desperately lamenting:

"No, no, no, *Dios mío*, my God, no, you killed him God, my poor man's flesh. Why? Why? Why? I asked you for our daily bread and here it is. You let them kill my man. Thank you: oh, thank you, and bless you!"

He listened, entranced as he staggered, until he heard a deafening and heavy thud in his ear, accompanied by another flood of blood that spewed out of his face and heard the sharp sound of bells tolling destructively. He fell and knelt and the other man tumbled over as well and sat close to him on the ground, both of them in the same puddle of blood that was already mixing with the dirt, each still brandishing his machete and pounding with well aimed but decreasingly vigorous blows on the other's face and neck and chest, until they both collapsed. They lay on the ground looking up at the purple sky, now spasmodically jerking their weapons, each thinking the battle had been proudly won, feeling the other's dying breath amidst the wild cries of the multitude. They looked at each other for a moment as though up until that instant they had not even seen each other and it was then that the pride which had overwhelmed them vanished as suddenly as it had arrived. And they heard themselves whisper:

"*Matáme, 'manito, matáme.* Kill me, little brother, kill me."

She who held a calloused, begging hand in her own hands crawled with her children toward the side of their dead protector to restore it, placing it against the bleeding stump while the other man, unable to move any longer, rolled his eyes upward to look at her with a supreme intensity and wailed with almost as much fury as he had before, when the street had been empty and he had leaped across it with a purpose only dimly understood:

"Don't let the bastards make bandits and whores out of our children! You hear me, woman? You hear me?"

The woman looked at him with fear and repugnance, sobbing while she caressed the dusty and bloody chest of her dead man, without understanding the meaning of the words hurled at her, feeling that in his delirium he had confused her with another woman, perhaps his own wife.

It was then that her barefoot boy, the oldest of her children, silently tore the machete from the still grasping hand of his father and, with great effort, lifted the heavy, bloody weapon overhead with both hands, discharging it with all his strength between the dying eyes of his father's killer, giving free reign to his feverish vengeance.

The street slowly emptied; the whispering groups of shadows moved away from death. Some of those who had been too far away to see all the details of the fight, and a few latecomers, moved close for a while, loitering about, staring dumbly at the corpses and at the child who had just killed a man, while several policemen arrived and carried the nameless bodies into an ambulance, followed by the screams and cries of the woman and her children.

Tomorrow the mute graves will sink. Perhaps tomorrow the sky will lose its purple hue. Tomorrow, the vibrant hills will cast out onto the city two more widows and a dozen or so more orphans, new beggars turned lose in the city.

But in the meantime, the dogs will lick the crimson corners of the street with avid, thirsty tongues.

The recruit

In the village everyone knew him.

One day he disappeared when a patrol came to induct unwary peasants into the army. He had met the patrol at the outskirts of town and they took him even though he told them he was his elderly parents's only means of support; that without him they would be abandoned, at the mercy of old age. But the soldiers took him no matter what he said. His protests were not heard. When the army came to recruit, nothing could save the peasants or the Indians from being inducted against their will.

He was to walk for two days with his hands tied behind his back and a rope around his neck fastened to the saddle of a mule. In the mountains, before arriving in the city where the army barracks were located, he tried to escape but they chased him and after a few hours captured and beat him so severely that he lost his eight front teeth and was almost blinded by the kicking they inflicted upon his face. He was unable to open his purple and swollen eyes for a week. On the third day they took off the handcuffs and gave him a piece of hard bread and a bowl full of sweetened water, what they called *aguapanela*. For three weeks they left him lying in the darkness of the prison cell without any medical services in spite of his prolonged moaning. They promised to kill him as a traitor of his homeland if he ever tried to escape again.

He served four years in the army and at the end of his enlistment they allowed him to return to his village to pick up the thread of his life. All his front teeth missing as they left him, with several deep scars on his face, his skin weather-beaten by the scorching sun of entire months spent outdoors, he was drastically transformed. But those external changes were slight compared to those suffered by his character: the tortures of his escape and of the prison cell, the constant humiliation and the abuses by his superiors, the blind obedience he had to keep night and day and the interminable months of guard duty, had turned him into a mistrusting and suspicious man who frequently blinked as though he felt frightened and persecuted. There were other reasons why his metamorphosis had been so complete, reasons he tried to forget, events that haunted him in his nightmares. He had changed in body and in spirit so thoroughly that now, when he returned to his village, no one recognized him. He had changed totally.

As the bus that brought him from the city on the last leg of his return approached the village and he began to see again the familiar places of his childhood, a profound anxiety overtook him. Suddenly, as the bus entered the village, he got off without waiting for the vehicle to stop, as he had skillfully done during his adolescence, and sat down to watch those who came to the marketplace, looking at the passers-by with his mouth wide open. No one recognized him. He did not dare speak to his acquaintances who now looked upon him with a certain amazement, as though they were in the presence of a ghost who made them feel slightly uneasy for some reason beyond their awareness. They looked upon him inquisitively, feeling there was something familiar about him, but when they saw how disfigured he was and his military shirt, they avoided him, deflecting their gaze awkwardly, almost certain they didn't know him. And he behaved in a strange way toward them as well: if someone stopped to look at him, he withdrew and looked in the opposite direction, fearful that they would recognize him. He didn't know whether he wanted to be recognized or not.

Slowly, he began to walk the length of the main street that would lead him toward the hut that had been his home for the first seventeen years of his life, looking with fascination at all the streets and houses that were so well known to him, cautiously coming close to the various groups in front of the taverns.

He thought of asking about his parents, but the anxiety he felt did not permit him to do so. Instead, he went near the groups without speaking, to find out whatever he could about the last four years of life in the village. He was not in any hurry. He had nothing else to do. Nevertheless, this freedom also made him feel oppressed. And he realized, with a certain sadness he could not decipher, that he was not only pretending to be a stranger but, after all his suffering and his prolonged absence, he was a stranger among his old neighbors. He felt as though he had never lived in this little village he knew so well, as though he had never listened to the *bambucos* of the sugar mills that were played by the bohemian guitars of the tillers with pouch and poncho, or known the peaceful afternoons after the laborious working day in the furrows of their mountains.

He thought he might be able to hear a reference to the happenings of four years before and in that way, without asking for it directly, be able to gather the fragments of his life which had been uprooted and perhaps feel again as he had before, be able to recover what he had lost.

He felt a remote melancholy -as though it were not his own sadness but that of the entire village- which momentarily and without apparent reason made him think of the resounding echoes of an ancient axe his father had used many years before in the forests of the hillsides. A vague sadness he was unable to understand or express in words, but which hindered him like a knot in his heart, or a foggy veil before his eyes; or perhaps more like a barrier inside of his being which imprisoned him and led him toward a path he did not wish to follow.

Little by little he pieced together the fragmentary bits of conversations he overheard, words flowing inevitably in mournful murmurs, barely reaching his ears, but which he captured in their full significance: fear of poverty and of abuse from the authorities had replaced the old ways; the army was bent on subduing them under any pretext; and the overwhelming increment in the cost of daily life transformed agrarian labor into a heartless and backbreaking toil which was more akin to slavery than to honest work and which now was a constant affront to the sentiment of dignity that had always been an inextricable part of their existence. The villagers had lost the pride with which, even during very difficult times, they had used to overcome disappointment and adversity.

Everywhere he heard the same story, the same complaints. And he found everywhere the desire to escape, to leave the village in search of better fortune, to abandon everything behind and forget, and to take the road toward the industrial centers in the crowded cities where they might be able to preserve a shred of dignity in the midst of the anonymity of the crowd, away from prying eyes.

Much to his sorrow, instead of the peaceful days of his childhood, he found only anguish.

Each time he captured a piece of some conversation, the knot he felt in his heart tightened, the tears flooded his eyes and the barrier inside his being cornered him with increasing power until he again felt like a prisoner, worse than he had felt during the years in the army. Because, after all, this was his village and here he had come to pick up the thread of his life. But now that all these people were saying that it was no longer worthwhile to continue living in the town, repeating here and there that life had become unbearable under the conditions of misery in which they found themselves, he felt completely disappointed.

His anger was difficult to overcome and incited him to walk faster in the direction of the hut where he had lived for so many years. He walked through familiar streets that led him to the other side of the village where every stone of the road seemed like a living memory from the past. He moved cautiously at first as though an enemy might be present, even though the streets were almost deserted. Once in a while, as he moved away from the center of the village, one or another house still exhibited the violent marks of plunder and at times the ruins, the mute rubbish which nevertheless screamed of nights in flames and of the death of innocents, with only the cruel wreckage as witnesses. He accelerated his step, but upon coming closer to the place where long ago he had dreamed of becoming a man, an unutterable knowledge was hurriedly formulated in his thought, and the certainty that he would never see his parents again began to torment him.

He thought of the little hut with the two rooms, so fragile and so poorly furnished that its existence could have been undone in a matter of minutes and all vestiges of those who had lived there and the objects used by his ancestors, erased during a short storm of violence, in a momentary shaking of agony followed by a sepulchral silence. He knew well that shaking and that silence. A chill overwhelmed him when he began to feel a furious rush of memories which he tried vainly to put out of his mind by brusquely shaking his head as if wishing to tear out of his brain the images of cruelty and violence of the last four years of his life.

At last he arrived at the place where he should have found that intimate reality of his childhood, the humble structure that could perhaps still save his life, but instead of the hut he expected to see again, there was nothing more than tall grass and he realized inescapably that his ominous premonition was like a fatal arrow headed straight to its mark.

He closed his eyes when he saw the grass was already taller than himself on the piece of land where his home should have been. Then he bent down fearfully and began to search among the grassroots until he found pieces of scorched wood. And as he desperately unearthed the burnt fragments already half-rotted and corroded by time and worms, the debris of what had been the dwelling of his childhood, those memories of his years in the regiment which he had tried in vain to exorcise from his mind -the experiences which had truly transformed his life more so than the beating he had suffered- finally invaded him.

Yes, he too had done damage equal to the one he now witnessed. He had followed orders to kill the innocents, the children of muleteers and peasants; to harm other Indians, calling them bandits or *guerrillas* or communists, as it was the custom in order to justify their slaughter, when in reality they were the opponents of the regime defended by the uniformed mob, hidden in the homes of the townsfolk who risked their lives protecting them. And too often they were only children. He too had been an accomplice in the national fratricide committed in the provinces which now was a part of the constant worry that propelled the people from the countryside to find refuge in the cities.

In the beginning, after he was tormented by his superiors, he felt forced, but later he participated in the campaigns without repugnance, without even thinking, as if it were an everyday happening; taking jubilantly the scarce booty of others's wealth which, after all, was the only payment he received, feeling the imponderable satisfaction during the killing as he realized for the first time in his life that others were afraid of him. And he remembered the pride he felt after so much humiliation and deprivation when they gave him the uniform in which he would become the living incarnation of the dread he would inspire and which, for a poor man like himself, had been the only way to win a crumb of respect and importance among men.

He continued scraping the ground with ever increasing eagerness which was transformed into vehemence when he found a piece of burnt stick that had been half buried in the ground's decay and which finally he recognized as one of the legs of the old family bed, the one used by his ancestors, where his parents had conceived him and where he was born, where they had protected him from the cold with their warm bodies during the winter nights of his childhood, where his parents had slept together through the twenty thousand nights of their lives before they were taken by surprise and annihilated. But just as he realized what he held in his hand, he flung that piece of wood from his past with loathing, vomiting a sour and thick substance which tasted like salt and rotten blood and seemed to come out in uncontrollable waves more from the depth of his soul than from the overwrought sinuosities of his intestines. In this manner, kneeling there, he sensed a cowardice about himself greater than any feeling he had ever experienced in his entire life, knowing that he too had inflicted comparable pain, that his parents had died in one of the thousand ways that his own tormentors had taught him to kill during the four years of service to his homeland.

He pulled himself away from the refuse where he found himself and began to run, thinking that he did not wish to know the details of what had occurred, disposed now not to approach those who had been his neighbors for many years.

He wished to live and die at the same time and did not know how to do one or the other. He felt the necessity to survive like the animal whose biological destiny was to continue breathing so that his own species among the other animals of the planet would not become extinguished. And at the same time he struggled with the unstoppable wish to die so he would not have the opportunity to resolve the hatred that gnawed inside him and be able to feel the sublime love that always could transform him into a being exquisitely vulnerable and sensitive to the smallest depredation.

In the midst of this silent conflict, his steps took him to the church, behind which was the cemetery, mechanically and automatically, as he had been taken there so many times during the years of his childhood and as he had been taught to march in the regiment.

He thought of seeing whether his parents were buried there and in this way at least bring a closure to that part of his life. He buttoned up the collar of his military shirt. His almost martial step made him remember the many marches toward distant and defenseless villages with a rifle on his shoulder. And he felt as though he were again under the orders of a superior; and that act, being so akin to obedience brought him a certain calmness, making him feel like he didn't have to continue thinking about impossible decisions which wore him out.

Once he arrived at the cemetery behind the church he walked with precision toward the high vaults where the tombs of the poor were marked on the lime walls. The number of the dead had grown recently.

He examined in silence the names of hundreds of people he had known, people who had been his friends. Half the world he had loved was now cloistered in these mute walls with their interminable rows of tombs.

At last, his inquisitive look stumbled upon the names of his parents, engraved on the highest row. They had received at least holy burial in exchange, most likely, for their small parcel of land no one had claimed. One was next to the other, the same date of expiration on both tombs. And knowing now with certainty the kind of death that must have seized them at the same hour, he suspected that those burned and gnawed fragments which scarcely remained of the fragile memories of his childhood would be transformed in a few instants into ashes which the most ephemeral breeze would sweep toward the inaccessible places of his being where they would remain buried and forgotten like a happy dream that was violently interrupted during the first dawn of his life when memories were still impossible.

Only for an instant did he fix his eyes upon those names which already appeared alien and which had not left any other trail upon the earth, and on that date which would remain anonymously suspended in the wall as an insignificant fragment in the immensity of time.

Those who saw him come out of the cemetery in front of the church were aghast as they beheld him because he walked as though he were bewitched, as though he moved under the scrutiny of some harsh general reviewing his troops. His eyes were fixed in the distance and he was deaf to every stimulus except for that interior purpose which obeyed an invisible force propelling him like a puppet.

It was then, the moment he left behind that row of tombs, when everything tying him to the village disappeared, when he felt inside his head the sudden arrival of a terrifying emptiness which separated him from everything he had known and was real to him, that the village was converted into ice and glass, with streets and houses that were square, rectangular, sharp-pointed, parallel, rectilinear; when all the forms straightened out, becoming perpendicular, triangular and remained inflexible, unbending, without any hint of roundness; when colors vanished and the whole universe was reduced to the variations between black and white.

Everything froze and became slippery like a mirror reflecting itself; inhuman and distant. The village was a desert without sands; glossy, rigid. The trees remained static, the wind stopped blowing, nothing seemed to move although men walked and children and dogs ran as they had always done, but now they remained suspended without reaching their goal, like in an interminable nightmare.

He didn't look at anyone but sensed that all the people were objects who had also lost one of their dimensions. What they lacked now was depth: they were long and broad, rectangular, but the third dimension had disappeared. Their bodies were made of plaster, of clay, of lime. Everything was about to break and crumble.

From the trees, insipid fruits were hanging. In the sky, the clouds had turned into parallel rivers of white blood; puddles of gray blood stagnated, and seas of black blood were agitating.

Everything was petrified in what to him became the mirage of the village. He stood in the middle of the park in front of the church in a posture of military attention, as though he were waiting for a superior to put him at ease but unable to do so by himself. The whole village was perplexed by his unusual conduct. He remained in that position of statue the rest of that day and the whole night, without eating, without attending to his physical needs until dawn, when the villagers ran terrified, fleeing from the platoon of soldiers that had entered the town again to recruit whomever they could catch, as was their custom, among the unwary peasants, to gather as many helpless Indians as possible.

The old men, the women and children who did not need to escape said that when the soldiers who saw him standing in the middle of the park in his rigid posture came close to him, he greeted them in perfect martial form with an impeccable military salute, in accordance with the best possible training, and they say that they heard him say only three laconic words, firmly, convincing, the only words he had uttered during his entire stay in the village: "I will obey!" He then followed the leaders voluntarily, helping them in their tasks as if he had always been a soldier and would always remain one.

The last time they saw him he was lost in the ranks of the uniformed army which, with their many new recruits, youngsters, peasants and Indians from the countryside who walked with a rope tied to their necks and attached to the saddle of a mule, was headed toward the army headquarters in the outskirts of the city.

The beggars

From the womb of the tattered woman, the creature could not see the distant light of stars. And the rest of the children, their glances distorted by hunger, were too sleepy and busy walking down the hill. The smallest one was carried by her mother, wrapped in a black mantilla that hung from the woman's back while one of her siblings could barely walk with his uncertain steps, grasping desperately at the protecting skirt, crying with a hoarse moan as though he had been crying this way from the hour of his birth.

To appease him the mother searched in a bag dangling around her neck and pulled out a piece of brown sugar loaf which she placed in his mouth. But in spite of the hunger he had and how much he liked the sweet treat, the movements of the mother were so brusque that she only was able to aggravate the desperation of the small one. Finally she gave up and let him continue moaning while he devoured the brown sugar.

The other three boys walked by the side of the woman downhill without her help among the ruinous shanties, huts and caves where the swarm of those who were forsaken lived. The mother and the three eldest boys pushed a single-wheeled pushcart that had been laboriously worked over to make it look like a primitive wheelbarrow. Another child, covered with newspapers and dirty rags, was lying on the rusted cart. It was difficult to discern in the shadows of dawn the age of this small one. Even when the light of day, when the glory of the sun illuminated the valley in such a way that no longer could anything lend itself to be confused with some hallucinated vision, the age of that child remained fathomless. For the time being he slept under the rags and his head moved from side to side, bobbing up and down, as though it were inert, marking the sudden beat of each turn of the irregular and shrill wheel. Sometimes it seemed like a jolt of the wheelbarrow would heave him upon the clumps of earth mixed with humid clay where they slid, or upon the hostile stones of the road. In spite of the constant jolts, he continued sleeping innocently with the tired and profound sleep of those who have entrusted their lives to another's destiny. Sometimes he seemed ready to wake up, holding his breath for a long time and then moving one or another extremity in a vague gesture of self-protection as though trying to embrace himself. But soon, he'd stop moving and resume the heavy breathing with a thick groan.

This way they came down into the city where the streets were deserted, with the nocturnal silence still dangling from the last stars. But as they approached the central plaza where the majesty of the cathedral rose toward the sky forming an enormous silhouette against the dawn, the eager blossoming of a new day forced them to hurry.

Today was the first day of the carnival and many people would come to commemorate the founding of the city. Strangers would come from lands beyond the seas. The activities of this day would climax when the archbishop would take out of the cathedral upon his shoulders a large golden vessel containing holy water to bless the frolicking costumed dancers and the monument to heroes in the square in a public demonstration of gratitude to the memory of the two conquerors who died for the Christian faith nearly five hundred years ago.

If she could only obtain a good place next to the main portal of the cathedral, where everyone entering had to pass, good fortune would perhaps smile upon her and her starving children. She was glad when the first rays of the sun, undisputable god of the firmament, focused upon her family and the cart, knowing that it would illuminate cruelly each piece of rag they were forced to wear, all the ravages of tiredness revealed in the emaciated flesh, the ineluctable signs of hunger: that fierce adversary who tormented them.

It wasn't until later, when at last they settled next to the wide portal of the cathedral, ready to be seen by everyone coming in and going out, that upon the insistence of the mother, each of the little ones thrust out the hand enslaved by poverty to make the universal gesture of the beggar. She then removed the dirty rags and the newspapers covering the creature in the wheelbarrow, to allow the solar light to reveal the dreadful spectacle now contorting in the reflexive movements of nerves and flesh and bones that shook without reason, appendices of impotent extremities which in their awkwardness mocked the human life that still seemed trapped and immutable in the anguished eyes of the being whose enormous hydrocephalic head occupied the greater portion of the wheelbarrow. The child's head -appearing all the larger because the rest of his body was so thin- resembled a colossal stone carved out to look like an infant's face, a relic rescued from the debris of rudimentary vestiges of some primitive tribe that ceased to exist long ago.

"Small alms, *por el amor de Dios*, for the love of God," the little children called out in unison.

"*Por el amor de Dios*, to calm the hunger," they repeated.

They grouped themselves on both sides of the portal, forming two rows between which the devout early risers walked in order to enter the cathedral. At the end of this corridor of begging children was the pushcart with the abnormal child with the fixed and desperate eyes twitching unconsciously. There he was, exhibited like the macabre painting in the gallery of horrors of some master maddened by his fury against an unjust society, next to the mother who once in a while cleaned the spittle oozing by the corners of his open mouth where already the tenacious flies of the new day had begun to prey.

She picked him up out of the cart and placed him on her lap as she sat against the brick wall of the magnificent structure because she knew that if she could exhibit wisely the monstrosity that wriggled there for everyone to see, now spread across her arms and bosom, she could create such a profound impression among the faithful that the image would grow in their vision and remain with them for the whole hour the Mass lasted. She hoped and prayed for their hearts to soften enough to reduce any resistance they might have to give alms, dislodging little by little the rancor they might hold feeling the intrusion of the needy ones who begged and of this incredible scene in a fresh morning which should be a delightful preamble for the joy of the carnival, at a time when they did not wish to know about the misfortune of others. She abstained from looking at them as they filed by her through the portal because she knew they would notice more the monster she held if they thought no one was watching them, if they felt alone contemplating misery without witnesses, without the look of adults they could interpret as recrimination. She knew that the more they looked at him the more irresistibly the image would become recorded in their memories. And she knew for certain that, once properly displayed and without being watched by her, they would have to satisfy their morbid curiosity and keep looking at the deformities. For a moment, a surge of having a bit of power over the onlookers invaded her. Later, when they would leave, she would nail her anguished eyes upon them, accusatory and imploring at the same time, when she would have her opportunity to trap the elusive coins. While she waited, she listened to the noise of the nascent city down there in the plaza where the daily concerns of a life that seemed to elapse in a world so different from her own, a life foreign to her experience, making her feel alien in her own land, like an unwelcome guest, as if none of the beauty there belonged to her, as though she had no right to participate in this life which after all was the only one she would have.

She looked at the people bedazzled, forgetting for a few minutes the mission occupying her, her position in this world, and remained absorbed noting the marvelous facility in the movements of those milling about far down in the plaza, seeing how they laughed with such ease, observing the manner in which they enjoyed the new day. But as she began to feel in her reverie a small bit of the exuberance that was present in the plaza, some fragment of the morning's energy surrounding her, she suddenly felt the sharp pain of hunger in her stomach and the jerking of her intestines stretching in an internal convulsion upon lacking anything to feed itself. Her stomach emitted a prolonged growl. She realized once more that all these strangers were inaccessible, immune to her pain, as though their entire lives were concentrated only on festivities and monies to spend, as though everything were so easy that one would only have to think of this or that to possess it freely, throwing away money that ran in torrents from hand to hand, redeeming bills that always circulated outside of her reach and with which she could obtain food to save her whole family.

She heard again the groans of the little one and unwrapping the last bits of brown sugar from her bag, she apportioned what was left of the loaf among the children who surrounded her immediately to receive the sweet they avidly devoured as they returned to their begging posts.

She suspected that the kind of happiness unfolding around her would never be part of her family's life as long as they had to depend on charity or the laws made by the owners of the city, and that by just asking nicely they would never have the right to live a peaceful life without the continuous and overwhelming violence of this terrorizing poverty.

Her face hardened again and she turned it toward those inside, banishing the momentary dream, the hope, narrowing her eyes and adopting a rigid posture as if she were trying to disappear somewhere where she would not need food to survive.

The priest's voice from the pulpit reached her vaguely. "Place your children's future in the hands of heaven and you will be taken care of," he preached. She looked vacantly in his direction with a slight smile of doubt on her lips. She had heard the admonition ever since she could remember and had trusted to no avail. She moved her head from side to side and shrugged her shoulders, mumbling.

She always thought about receiving more that what they ever gave her. She remembered a day long ago when she was a child and her family was invited into the large house of a wealthy man who took pity on them. There, behind the high iron gates which protected the mansion, they ate amply until they were filled. They could even take a few bowlfuls of leavings for the next day. Now, she swallowed saliva.

After the Mass ended and all the people had left, the beggars moved to a shadier spot by the sidewall of the cathedral. After four hours of begging they still had not collected enough coins to calm their hunger and they were exhausted, with hardly enough vitality to extend their hands toward the hated giver.

As they received some alms, the mother would send the oldest of her children to buy food for the small ones, but so little could be purchased that it was impossible to feed all of them. As the hours passed the internal contortions occurred with greater frequency.

"Don't you dare spend those coins on foolishness, you hear me? It's to buy milk for the little sick one."

But when the ill child with the extraordinary head felt upon his lips the contact of a warm bottle and intuitively realized they were trying to feed him at last, he desperately began to choke with the milk. In his greedy desire to consume everything at once, before one of the others could take the bottle away from him -even though the mother was always defending the sick one- he began to vomit everything he had already consumed.

"He don' like milk '*amá*,'" said one of the children.

And feeling he had the right to the bottle because his sick brother had failed to drink, he snatched it away before the rest of the contents would go to waste and ran away with it, sucking it, laughing while he drank the milk in great gulps, chased by two of his brothers and by his mother's scolding shouts.

They continued begging through the sweltering afternoon. Once in a while, the mother and the eldest of her sons wished to feed the sick one who kept trying to move his head but could barely do so, trying to help himself like a wounded animal, blurting out with great effort some incomprehensible complaint. He ate with an uncommonly large covetousness but shortly after swallowing whatever they gave him, he vomited and moaned again.

The other children ran through the park after having eaten a few crumbs, competing with each other in searching the garbage cans where they found something to carry away like a trophy, but which in reality amounted only to a piece of discarded meat or a half rotted fruit, picking up cigarette butts which they finished smoking with deep puffs as though these too were food to sustain life.

They ran recklessly through the park interrupting conversation as they begged, making transient friendships with other children in the same condition.

Seeing a well-dressed elderly lady carrying a purse in an isolated place behind the cathedral, three of the brothers pushed her against the wall and snatched the purse from her, leaving the lady moaning painfully on the street. They searched the purse after disappearing around the corner, taking out its insignificant trinkets and a few small bank notes and coins which they kept gleefully, then threw away the empty purse into a hole of the sewage system below. When they returned to their mother they bragged, showing her the bills proudly. And they ran to the market and bought a great variety of all sorts of cheap food and fruits which they carried in a paper bag.

The mother suspected they had taken the money illicitly, not by begging, but asked nothing of them. Each member of the family except the sick one chose what to eat and did so until satiated, leaning against the discolored wall of the cathedral, forgetting the sick one who had lost all desire for food, burning with fever, self-absorbed in his own suffering.

Slowly it began to darken and the cold air of the mountains descended to the city. For warmth, the smallest children huddled next to their mother who sustained the sick one in her arms, covering herself with a few sheets of the days's news that now were old, while the three bigger ones, feeling a new sense of camaraderie through the violent theft they shared, settled in an embrace on a large piece of cardboard they placed on top of the iron grill of the sewage system through which escaped a fetid but warm subterranean air emanating from the entrails of the city. Trusting, they surrendered to sleep, the three urchins who had tasted the illusory and transient gratifications of delinquency, the three loitering little beggars whose contribution to the future was sealed, irrevocably determined by their short past. But upon awakening, those children of the dawn felt anew the first omens of the hunger of the new day, the familiar emptiness in the stomach that only food would soothe.

They began again to beg on that second day of the carnival as their mother had done even before the days of giving them birth.

She had tried to feed him when he awoke but the sick child did not show any interest and closed his mouth. Breathing had become difficult and he emitted a few hoarse sounds each time he inhaled, attracting greater attention. The coins today were filling the tin can faster. She held it out in her trembling hand, making the coins sound like a rattle even though it wasn't her purpose to make such a discordant sound. She seemed to be in a hurry looking eagerly at each person walking by her side. With the other hand she cleaned the feverish sweat from the child's face and swatted at the insatiable flies. Several times she emptied the tin can and hid the coins. They give more during a carnival when they're feeling happy, she mumbled. The hiding of the coins was done surreptitiously, afraid that if they'd find out how well she was doing today they would stop giving to her. The coins were hidden in a bag that hung from her neck under the dirty mantilla, anxiously counting them first to make sure they were not inventions of her imagination. She stopped looking at the child in her arms and devoted all her attention to the coins and the people who began to surround her.

She knew exactly the moment when the child in her arms died.

The enormous head unhinged itself upon her dry breast. The coarse sound of his breathing remained suspended and he slowly exhaled a warm air that left his chest flat. Those eyes which had searched the skies of his homeland hardened. A viscous and pale cover blinded them forever.

But the mother pretended not to be aware and continued exhibiting him for days after the child ceased breathing, clutching the coins voraciously, thinking about the survival of her other children, until a putrid odor began to come out of that inert and cold body which she could no longer keep warm no matter how hard she tried. Because the stench scared them and made them gag, the other children moved away frightened, leaving the mother alone with the child decomposing in her arms, surrounded by onlookers with handkerchiefs pressed against their noses.

The priest

Although he was the parish priest of the lowlands, neither the ecclesiastic nor the civilian authorities informed him of the transformations that would take place in the barrio.

When his neighbors came to tell him that the lowlands would become a red-light district, he could not believe the news. But a few hours after the decree regarding the streetwalkers appeared, the women began to arrive in the district by the hundreds. He saw them loitering in the streets, many of them lying aggressively on the grass in the empty lots between houses. The music from the taverns, with its pulsating and deafening beat, invaded the peacefulness of the chapel and the adjacent room he occupied, and the priest felt frustrated not knowing how to defend his poverty-stricken parishioners.

He prayed devoutly before doing anything else, as was his custom, making promises to God he was sure he could keep in exchange for divine assistance. He surmised that he would need much help in this matter because it was something he couldn't understand and was completely outside the problems he was used to solving. He decided to sacrifice for a whole year his weekly visits to his secular home— his family's mansion on the other side of the city—,promise God he would abstain from the pleasure of spending time with his parents. This was the home where he had spent his life in the lap of luxury until the day he entered the seminary and where he loved to go for a rest when his ecclesiastic duties became overwhelming. He went there to protect himself from the hardships of his vocation.

He prayed for a whole hour, a little annoyed that the music didn't stop and peace was not restored. He was a gentle man whose words brought a great calm to the needy families of the neighborhood and whose generosity toward the poor was thoroughly acknowledged in the parish.

He shook his head, pained because the problem had not vanished. So often, difficulties were resolved just as he had asked, almost miraculously. But God knew his heart better than he knew himself, he thought, closing his eyes again.

Perhaps this tribulation would unexpectedly become a test of faith. If he at least could pray well, if his words had the eloquence of the great saints of the Church, if his phrases were as erudite as those of a sage, or as sublime as those of a poet, perhaps they would penetrate that termite-eaten roof, would scurry among the leaves of the trees and, rising above the clouds, arrive straight at the very throne of God to be heard above all this infernal music which didn't even allow him to think. And wouldn't it be wonderful if his words could change what the city had ordered? Turn events around and restore the peace of the barrio?

Maybe he shouldn't make offers to his God: Will you give me this if I sacrifice that? His confessor had chided him gently for trying to make deals with God during his seminary days. It was a bad habit, a foolish reaction when he felt helpless. He was a man now, he told himself. But what harm was there in making promises, especially ones he could keep. For a long time he had fulfilled every promise he had made to God in his supplications. He wouldn't let himself forget the last time he had disappointed his God with an unkept promise.

The incident happened during the year after he entered the seminary as a young man just out of high school many years ago, before his final examinations. He hadn't been able to keep his promises and he got sick with intermittent fevers which no physician could diagnose. Sporadic attacks of diarrhea left him completely exhausted and unable to sleep for weeks. He considered himself divinely punished and he never broke a promise to his God after that experience. Keeping promises became one of his most sacred private laws; his personal pact with God, he thought proudly. And now, when he heard the reckless yells from the street surging repeatedly with renewed vigor like the waves of an irrepressible tide, he wondered whether he should offer another sacrifice, enlarge his part of the bargain.

He plugged his ears with cotton and closed his eyes, wishing with all his powers of concentration that the unleashed evil against his parish would disappear. But the cotton was not enough to restore the blessed peace he was used to have in the quiet neighborhood of honest workers. He could still hear the strident music that vibrated with a confused and wanton pattern in which the savage and lascivious pulsations of several different rhythms were aimlessly mixed. Yes, he must pray more, sacrifice something that would truly hurt him, something that would be anchored in the very depths of his being and which would mark his life irreparably.

He felt the edge of a nail sticking into his skin as he knelt before the huge crucifix and he hoped that God would surely see and take pity on his pain, that He would appreciate his sacrificial tribute and help him solve the problem. For a moment he forgot about the commotion outside as he drove his knee against the nail until he felt the flow of blood.

When his parishioners came into the chapel he was still kneeling, crossing himself now and then. They waited impatiently at a distance, shifting their weight from one foot to the other restlessly, coughing to get his attention because they didn't dare to call him. He knew they were waiting for him, that they would ask for his help, and he felt distressed at not knowing what to do. But his intentions were good and he was a charitable man.

He thought God would help him at the decisive moment, that He would give him strength of spirit and understanding, that in the next instant he would receive divine inspiration.

He would have liked to remain kneeling all day and night, feeling the cruelty of the piercing nail mortifying his knee instead of facing the overwhelming demands of his congregation. He thought of the saints who sacrificed their lives for noble causes and for a moment wished to die crucified with Christ, and told himself that if the opportunity were offered he would gladly give his life to lessen in the slightest the pain suffered by his Savior.

They began to call his name, at first under their breath and when they received no answer, summoned their courage until a murmur of voices clamored for his attention:

"Father! Father! Come help us!"

It was then he felt obligated to suspend his bargaining with God in order to escape the present reality. He got up and came close to them, pretending to be sure of himself, not aiming to deceive them, just looking at them paternally to instill courage and hope. As he approached, they surrounded him submissively, kneeling as they had always done to ask his blessing.

After they received the blessing one of the men stood up. "What shall we do, Father?" the man asked. "The authorities decided to turn our homes into houses of prostitution. They are trying to force us to sell our homes, *Padrecito*. It's all we have. We built the houses with our own hands and with what they pay for them now we couldn't buy another house anywhere else in the city. Help us stop them, Father. What can we do if they kick us out? And where will we go? Who will protect us?" The others listened in silence, nodding their heads from time to time, the women crying, moving their lips in continuous prayer, passing trembling fingers over their rosaries.

"Faith, hope and charity," the priest told them, "are the qualities of the good Christian. But above all, my children, we must have faith: faith in God and in the Holy Church. We will always receive divine protection if our faith remains." And before they had the chance to make another demand, he led them to the altar kneeling again, searching with his knee for the consoling and cruel head of the nail and praying loudly this time, trying to drown out the sound of the pagan music from the street.

His parishioners knelt around him, hoping for his special powers to come forth, expecting some supernatural force to save them from the injustice hanging over their humble neighborhood, reverently believing that if anyone could help them, this priest would somehow do it. For they remembered the many times he had come to console them in the depth of the interminable night of sickness or when death had visited them. Kneeling there, with the light from the altar plainly on his face, he looked like one of the saints pictured on the sheets distributed during the catechism hour. By the altar's light, with his high-pitched voice that couldn't hide the fear stalking him, the priest appeared even younger than he was. Seeing him this way they realized his fragility, how afraid he was. But, somehow, he would help them now, since he had always understood their suffering and had advised them with care and compassion. The priest looked at them realizing his impotence in this incomprehensible situation which was as new for him as it was for everyone else, something his teachers in the seminary had never taught him to resolve.

He felt saddened because he knew he must give them some kind of counsel, and he didn't have the faintest idea how to lessen their difficulties nor did he know the path to guide them. He continued praying, watching his flock surreptitiously, observing how the majority of the women, dressed in black, kissed the floor as they knelt. The men standing, holding their hats in their hands with their ponchos carefully folded over their shoulders, formed a line, looking ready to wage a battle. A few of them knelt with bowed heads and reverent expressions or with a supplicant look fixed on the purple wounds of the crucified Christ. The priest remembered tenderly the ideals of youth, the constant yearning of his childhood and adolescence to become a priest in the midst of a flock of penitents, surrounded by their love, confident that he would help them find the road to salvation.

He looked again and saw the living reality of everything he had waited for during his formative years. But this was different. This was more related to man's laws than to God's. He longed for a yesterday that would never return.

A bus filled with women stopped in front of the chapel. When the women were got off, their savage and profane screams assaulted the priest's ears, suddenly bringing him out of his self-absorption and reminding him of the necessity to take action. After he finished praying, the man who had spoken before said:

"Father, some of us organized a neighborhood committee this morning to ask the government its reasons for choosing our barrio as a haven for prostitutes and they told us that since most of those living here have not been legally married and live without the Church's blessing, they are—that is, we are—as sinful as any of the women of the happy life who sell their flesh in the streets. What do you say, Father?"

He had forgotten that detail, and hardly heard the question. Yes, it was true that the majority lived in sin because their union had never been sanctified by the sacrament of matrimony. It had never occurred to him because he had baptized so many children and buried so many of the old people who died in his parish. But it was the truth; they lived in sin without the indispensable blessing of the Church.

After so many years of living together they felt ashamed to ask the priest to marry them in the Church, after so much shared life. It was better not to speak of it. But now, the priest realized the majority of his parish had lived in sin for all those years before his very eyes. He never thought of them as being sinful. He grieved, feeling a heaviness burden his heart, and he asked himself if he had fallen short in his obligations. Perhaps he was responsible.

"Oh, my children," he said, "the ways of God are mysterious. We never know what his plans are for us, his poor servants, his flock. We are all sinners. I will always be ready to bless those who wish to consecrate their marriage at any time, day or night. Perhaps once your union is sanctified they will leave you alone."

Three hundred and fifty five couples from the lowlands neighborhood -many with grown-up children and grandchildren present- gathered at the chapel to be married and blessed by the priest that same evening, but the wheels of injustice had made their inexorable move and there was no way to stop the authorities. Although he was thanked by his parishioners for his good will, they continued asking him to help them in more active ways, promising to be better Christians in the future. The priest blessed them again, saying, "We must not doubt God's plans. I am nothing more than a poor priest who loves all of you."

It was easy for them to see he was honest and that his heart was with them. But the man who had spoken before raised his voice again for the third time, saying, "Our Father, we ask you to join our committee and go with us to the governor's palace. We don't think it's fair that our homes be sold under duress for the pleasure of harlots and the business of pimps. Surely God is with us. We are working families. If you and the Church would join us they would stop tormenting us. We ask the Church to help us change this new law, put the women somewhere else if they have to have their red-light district. Not where our children are growing up. Come with us in our march, Father. Help us."

"I will help you the best I can," he answered. "But before joining your march I must ask the bishops's permission. In the meantime I will remain here for you. God will help us."

Realizing he was disappointing them, he added, shaking his head, "It isn't easy for the priest of a poor neighborhood. My heart and my blessing are with you, my beloved people, but I must remain here until I hear from my superiors. They know best."

Suddenly, he seized upon an idea and added, "Would some of you help me carry a loudspeaker? We could make a bigger noise to drown out their confounded music and devilish screaming." Some of the more fervent parishioners smiled shyly, like children whose pranks have not yet dealt their full blow of mischief, whose powers are yet untested and, particularly the women and those who were more pious, offered their help in carrying out the priest's plan.

Those who left tried to understand the reasons given by the priest for not participating in their committee's actions, saying that after all, he could do no more for them without the support of his superiors. But the priest noticed that when the man who had spoken for the others knelt to receive the sacramental blessing, his face was taut. The priest sensed that the man's black eyes dared to search his own, plumbing the depths of his soul like no one had done before. And when the worker got up from his bent knee to leave, the priest saw that the man did not cross himself as was the custom and as the others did. But the priest had accepted long ago the vow of obedience to his superiors and knew he could not do what his heart dictated in such public matters, but had to wait for orders from his superiors before proceeding. He loved his people and didn't try to hide from the man's scrutiny.

The worker went out into the street knowing he had rebelled against the Church when he refused to cross himself, when he had dared to search for the truth in the priest's heart with an affront he hadn't suspected he could muster. He was still surprised that those eyes hadn't tried to deceive him, and that they had allowed him to look into the priest's most intimate being with a confidence and a love that now shamed him. That one is a good little priest, a good Father, the man thought, and I thought unfairly he was not to be trusted.

All day the priest and his helpers walked through the lowlands neighborhood as in a procession, carrying the images of saints on their shoulders while shouting prayers and admonitions into the loudspeaker in Spanish and a Latin that nobody understood, at best making only enough racket to drown out the music closest to them. But his momentary triumph brought him nothing but the ire of the women and their pimps, who began to ridicule him, shouting in their turn, the taverns turning up the music when he and his followers came near.

At the end of the day, he was hoarse and exhausted, frustrated by his lack of strength. He could barely speak. When he returned to his room, adjacent to the chapel, he had to listen all night to the furious shouting of those who came to wreak vengeance upon him for trying to oust them from the neighborhood. From time to time a rock would hit his door, startling him. The women took turns to ensure he wouldn't get any sleep, whispering vulgarities through the keyhole, trying to tempt him, offering themselves for his pleasure, saying to him repeatedly, "Under your cassock you must be a real man."

The priest heard them through the strongly bolted door in spite of having filled his ears with cotton and wrapped his head with a wool scarf given to him by an aunt for his last birthday when he became thirty-five years old.

The noise, the vengeful fury of those on the other side of the door, and his own anxiety wouldn't allow him to rest. Tears filled his eyes as he knelt with a prayer book and a crucifix in his hands, alone. He didn't want to believe that such was the evil of his childhood city where he had lived for years protected from the poverty and terror that were a part of it and which were now aligning themselves against him for the first time in his life. How was it possible that the poor people would lose the homes they built with their own hands only for having lived in sin without the Church's blessing. These workers and their families were his flock, his people, and he loved them even though they were sinners. There seemed to be no justice.

All night he cried and prayed while listening to the voices tempting him. Deep into the night, nearly overcome by the excitement and exhaustion of the last twenty-four hours he dozed while he prayed more calmly for the salvation of those who were plaguing him. But he woke again with the first light of dawn when he heard the murmuring of women's coaxing voices, feigning lust, calling for him beside his door. He didn't dare move, even though his body began to shake. And picking up the crucifix that had slipped off the couch with one hand and holding the prayer book with the other, he stopped his ears with his knuckles, shouting the new prayer to cast aside temptation, feeling a living fear of the spiritual danger that confronted him in his own flesh. When dawn arrived to rescue him, he begged some of his parishioners to take turns accompanying him, insisting that at least two of them stay with him wherever he went so that the women wouldn't torment him. They helped obediently, posting themselves much like guards by the closed door and chased the women away while he tried to sleep for a few hours unmolested by the drunken voices.

On the third day of the invasion, the community's school was closed by government decrees and the building converted into a clinic for the prevention of venereal diseases and a police station. Classrooms were turned into cells for prisoners on their way to the city's main prison.

Standing in front of what had been the school, the priest admonished the people to remember Christ's second coming and he blessed the children as they evacuated the building. Just as the school's director handed the keys over to the police commander in the presence of the whole community, a long-awaited messenger arrived with the bishop's orders which the priest proceeded to read aloud and which, after a long preamble, said that he should lend no aid to the neighborhood committee "because it is a group which unfortunately has been deceived and led astray by outside communist agitators whose intention is to destroy our democratic and Christian way of life."

The bishop directed him further by saying that the archbishop would be very pleased if he could organize a new committee of the faithful, a committee that truly represents the interests of the people in order to study the problems occurring in the neighborhood as reactions to the laws recently adopted by the Provincial Assembly.

He looked at the letter thoughtfully, wondering how he could carry out the task, and for a few seconds doubted the wisdom of the counsel he had just received, realizing that the strength of the neighborhood would be divided into two different factions, complicating the situation more than it was. He wondered where the outside political agitators referred to in the note had come from. He hadn't heard of anyone outside the community being involved in the lowland's problems. But surely his superiors had access to information beyond his reach. They always knew more than he did. Of course he would obey and do as they asked. And as he put aside his last doubts he felt a great relief at having a concrete sense of what he should do, of what was expected of him, and he felt comforted by the conviction that, as the Church's representative in the community, he would be prepared to help his people. He was ready to help them form another committee that would keep faith alive.

The priest began to recruit his most devoted assistants, reading them the bishop's message over and over and telling them it was like a voice from heaven calling on the chosen ones to unite in a just cause to change the entire course of their lives and inevitably bring them to God's very throne. And as the membership in the first committee shrunk as a result of his effort, the man who had refused to cross himself, came to speak with him again. This time the worker asked the priest not to disperse the scant forces of the earlier committee by creating a second one. "It creates a conflict, Father," he told the priest. "We are only a few."

The worker insisted but realizing his words were, as before, insufficient, he began to plead to no avail. As he turned away, feeling hurt in his disappointment, he again tried for the last time to scrutinize the priest's eyes, setting aside the shame and guilt. He found out that even though the priest's love and concern for his people remained, the priest's innocence had begun to disappear, dampening the glow of his youth.

In place of the vanishing innocence, the worker saw the dawning light of a new pride that might be transformed into the vain illusion of self-deceit, a strange light which from its nascent awakening was destined to blind the priest to his own self.

The priest was taking pleasure in the work he was carrying out for his superiors. Everyone could see he was indeed occupied with something urgent and responsible in helping the neighborhood families. A feeling of certainty about the virtuous intent of his mission came over him while he walked, followed by members of the new committee amid the raucous noise of the crowd. He was surprised to notice how his hand possessed a new self-confidence he had lacked before as he extended it to bless those who were kneeling, with an upward movement of the fingers which he now made a part of his blessing with extraordinary ease.

* * *

Many years later in the century of tragedies, several of the fearsome narcotraffickers and the members of the guerrilla whose aim was to bring down the government of millionaires, sprang from the barrio of the lowlands: children and grandchildren of those victimized by the resolution concerning public women.

A FEW CHARACTERS IN THE VILLAGE OF SANTA BÁRBARA

The serenaders

Don Alejandro had to borrow a pair of long trousers from his uncle Max, the major, since all the men in his home were shorter than he was. He was convinced that the serenaders of the village, three of the Cuervo brothers, would not take him seriously if he showed up in the short trousers of his adolescence to negotiate a contract with them.

He also suspected that they would not pay any attention to him if he dressed in the baggy trousers that reached down just above the calves where they were tied to the legs. Those became fashionable in the capital beyond the mountains and were worn by boys from more affluent families in the villages. But it was risky to use them because boys from poorer families who could not afford to buy what they called *pig-grabbing* trousers had spread a malicious rumor, saying that those who wore such garments defecated into them while standing. Don Alejandro put on the long pair of trousers that Don Maximiliano lent him, which, in spite of fitting his length, were so loose that he had to tighten his belt, jam together all the extra material and put on a poncho so that no one would notice the bunching up of his clothes. He walked over on a Saturday afternoon to arrange a performance by the three Cuervo brothers, who were singers and guitarists.

For fifteen cents each and a bottle of the local brandy called "ardent water" to warm their spirits and tune up their vocal chords, they performed the most romantic serenades of the entire region. Of course, there was no guarantee that they would not end up totally drunk. Quite the contrary, the surest bet was that even at the beginning of their concerts they would be well into their drinks, having started on their own bottles hidden under their ponchos. They just about promised and assured getting good and drunk. But Nicanor, Obdulio and Atanasio Cuervo considered themselves men of the world, in spite of never wandering outside of the province of Antioquia and neighboring Caldas. They swore that they would never commit indiscretions of any kind no matter how much of the brandy filled their bellies. And truly, that is how things went: all lit-up and staggering to the point of having to lean against the walls, for otherwise they might have rolled on down the hills, hardly able to open their eyes—much less maintain them focused—almost totally plastered, the Cuervo brothers always behaved like perfect gentlemen while they gave their monthly serenade to

Don Alejandro's girlfriend Evita, each one a virtuoso in his artistic specialty.

"The truth is," said Nicanor, who was in charge of the arrangements and was the one with an eye on the collective consumption of the drinks, "that without libations, or remaining dry while dealing with the outrages of a hangover after a good binge, our voices wouldn't even come out, remaining stuck inside in a most sickly way. Brandy not only animates, warms and cleanses our gullets, and—most importantly—our spirits, preparing the road so the sounds will emerge well from our stomachs, but also without it we would stay mute. It would be impossible to make the slightest harmonious sound."

Nicanor, as reveling night owl that he was, could have delivered erudite conferences in a grand manner at university lecture halls about the merits of his vice and that of his two colleague brothers, with a cornucopia of abundant physiological, chemical, genetic, philosophical reasons, and moreover as an expert in the principles and art of counterpoint, to convince the most incredulous. But, misguided or not, the whole neighborhood was a witness to the truth of the matter: the bigger the bender they sprung, the better their voices sounded, and with greater dexterity and subtlety they played any of their musical instruments. There was no doubt about it!

They communicated with each other with their eyes and through preconceived signals which, through daily usage and thousands of hours of rehearsals and performances together, had become incorporated into their character, transformed into subliminal signs that no one else was able to perceive, much less understand. Even when they could no longer speak, they wouldn't commit a single error singing, so much so that they no longer looked like three persons playing a concert, but one entity alone consisting of three bodies with three musical instruments.

"Now they're really playing full blast!" their excited spectators commented, poking each others' ribs with their elbows.

The three Cuervo brothers would climb the steep hills until they reached the top of the Street of Heights to give their serenade every time that Don Alejandro came for them, always ready to please not only his requests and those of Evita but the ones of his neighbors and cousins, the Peláez girls. They'd whisper the titles of their favorite songs through their windows until the performers would hear them.

The first serenade lasted from midnight till two o'clock in the morning, under an enormous and magnificent moon that seemed to smile at everyone, hiding playfully among the small clouds of the Andean summer, lighting capriciously the small stony street that snaked down to the middle of the village.

The good thing about the Cuervo brothers was that they not only knew by heart the complete string of *bambucos*, tangos, *pasillos* and boleros of those times, but all the varieties of popular songs of the hemisphere as well. They chose their programs for the serenades from this vast collection according to their own mood before and during their presentation, determined—it goes without saying—by the volume and quality of alcohol consumed.

Usually, they began to warm their fingers playing Evita's favorite song, *Ojos verdes* [Green eyes], that being the color of what she used daily with such dexterity to slaughter Don Alejandro and drive him crazy. But after playing songs like *Amapola, Ramona, Beautiful Dollie, Little Street Lamp, Gypsy Lament,* and the perennial *Antioqueñita*, which were the most liked songs at the time, they proceeded with their interpretations of special classical works which no one knew in those lands, like the *Spanish Dance* of Granados and also of Albéniz, the *Gallardas* of Gaspar Sanz, the *Sonatas* of Fernando Sor and the *Mazurcas* of Francisco Tárraga, showing off their skills and leaving their audiences completely overwhelmed. The more they drank -standing leaning, as the locals called it- the better they sounded. The people of Santa Bárbara were convinced, for good reasons, that their complete program could take its place among the best musical presentations even in the capital of the republic.

"They know more music than in Santafé de Bogotá," the peasants, wearing their long ponchos, would say, listening astounded, shaking their heads, eyes shut and frowning with supreme seriousness, as though they were offering the opinions of experts.

When the three Cuervo brothers became truly inspired—an event which commonly happened after they had ingested the whole bottle of ardent water brought by Don Alejandro—, they played variations of flamenco like *caña*. And when they were totally potted with the additional consumption of the liquors they had carried under their ponchos, they even dared to play compositions by Mozart, Chopin and Bach. It was at about that time when they would begin experimenting with new characteristics of sounds and gyrations of harmony that were original, often arriving at truly superhuman resonances.

Their reputation grew and the villagers, who hardly had heard any other kind of music performed, thought that the three Cuervo brothers must have been musical geniuses. And perhaps they were, because none of them had more education than the primary one that many in the village attained in those days, and the notions of basic music that they knew had been taught to them by their father, Don Emiliano Cuervo, who received at the age of twenty, a few solfeggio lessons toward the end of the last century from an itinerant Argentinian who claimed to have been a pianist at a pier restaurant of his beloved Buenos Aires and had exchanged a few months lodging in Don Emiliano's home for music lessons to the children in the family. The rest of the Cuervo family's musical knowledge was self-taught.

"If it weren't for the fact that we are hooked on brandy, drunkards without redemption but also without remorse, we would not be so brilliant," Atanasio proudly proclaimed with his mellifluous baritone voice and a sparkle of mischief in his pie-eyed look, glancing toward his brother Nicanor, who encouraged him with a beatific smile as he closed his eyes, assenting, knowing that his brother fed on his approval. Such was the most sublime of moments in their lives.

The two fools of Santa Bárbara

In the village there were no telephones and the postal service was slow and unstable. The villagers generally went to the fountain in the central park to send any news or information with the women who went there for water. But to relay a message, no matter how trivial, through that network of exaggerators and gossip mongers was to expose oneself before the whole world. To communicate during courtship, instead of using that headquarter of rumor spreaders, lovers engaged a different type of services.

It so happened that in the village there were two fools who competed with each other, offering themselves as messengers, pushing their way wherever there was a gathering, hoping to grab for themselves any measly loose penny. Although they lived in Santa Bárbara for many years, and were in the same communications business, as the two of them called their profession, there is evidence indicating that they were never seen together and many in the village claimed that they had never even spoken to each other. Both of them were originally from the town of Marinilla, known for the many enlightened souls it had given to the region in past years.

Ñoño dressed in the same Army uniform every day and lived obsessed with the military life, showing off with much relish a few medals he polished at all hours with the sleeves of his coat or shirt. He wore these decorations on his chest as irrefutable proof of having received the highest honor for his acts of bravery during the worldkiller battles of The War of One Thousand Days. He displayed his medals and ribbons to whomever might show some interest in taking a look at them and also uncovered the scars from several wounds which, according to him, he received defending human rights. He also bragged about having witnessed the treaty of Neerlandia that was signed in 1902, an event that nobody else had heard about.

Ñoño was an incurable, importunate beggar who nevertheless aroused compassion among the majority of the villagers. He used strategies that ranged from threats to whimpers in order to pick up errands, often demonstrating his firm conviction that he who doesn't cry doesn't get to suckle either. But he wasn't very reliable because his mania for boasting about his exploits in the military services deflected him from his focusing on work. He often stood around mooning away, waiting for flies to land, as they said. Or, perhaps he was pondering the merits of some military strategy. Another one of his qualities that retarded the chores he was supposed to carry out was his insistence in making out receipts for the pennies he received. He'd sign on any piece of paper available, on pieces of torn newspapers and he did it with phenomenal ostentation, as though he were a czar of industry. None of his signatures—illegible scribbles—resembled each other. If they refused to take his receipt, he'd start bawling. Of course, the majority of errands were forgotten and his mission would remain unfulfilled or indefinitely postponed. The pestering adolescents from the village, gangly beings without any other aim than to sour the lives of mankind, asked him on more than one occasion:

"Hey man, Ñoño, how's it that you whine so much being a veteran of The War of a Thousand Days? Soldiers don't cry. You, crying like a baby, for sure never was no soldier."

When he didn't know what to answer, they made a circle around him and tormented him yelling together like a choir:

"He who's a fool to Heaven can't go: screwed over here, there they'll say no!"

Another of the matters which sidetracked Ñoño was his infatuation over playing with his armies of little lead soldiers. He had two different troops: one was given to him by an uncle from Medellín during a visit and was made up of legionnaires—heartless mercenaries of the desert who specialized in ambushes—; the other, of Cossacks with a devastating cavalry and a platoon of sharpshooters with infallible aim, sold to him by one of the itinerant gypsies who came to town annually with his tribe of roaming circus performers.

Ñoño ordered his troops into combat on the uneven ground in the middle of Fountain Park, generally assuming absolute command over the Cossacks—dressed in red—whom he called his "fellow liberals."

He passed the time of day enraptured, completely self absorbed in his warring activities, issuing orders to underlings and threatening the enemy. "Let's follow the orders of General Rafael Uribe Uribe," he'd say in the middle of the fray. He'd grab one of the red lead soldiers and exclaim in martial tones:

"I order you to stop all the secret maneuvers of the enemy! And if you don't obey me, I'll send you to the dungeon even if you are a colonel! I don't care: to be a fool around here is no excuse!"

When the conflagration began, he threw sand on the army of legionnaires—dressed in blue, whom he called "the terrible conservatives"— and made fun of the little soldiers who fell from their posts during the frays:

"Stupid recruits, fools, fools, all of you, don't even know how to stand up. And don't come to me with your silly whining of weaklings because a good soldier don't cry; those who cry are fools, and he who's a fool to Heaven can't go: screwed here, over there they'll say no!"

Once he began his maneuvers with the little lead soldiers in the great battlegrounds of death, in the apocalyptic struggles he carried out daily, nobody could interrupt him and the errands would become, without doubt, insignificant details in the midst of important military decisions.

The townsfolk used to comment about Ñoño not being as much of a fool as people thought he was, but they were sure that at least a couple of roof tiles had moved out of place in his head. The most charitable ones— who knew him from the time he was a child—used to say that the contusions he suffered during one of the battles in The War of a Thousand Days had turned him topsy-turvy. They remembered him as an intelligent boy.

"That one's coconut skids," people used to say when Ñoño wouldn't hear them, making circles with their index finger around their own heads.

Since almost nobody used his services because he was so unreliable, he walked the streets like a dog without a master, most unkempt, and sometimes mortified people by intruding among them, insisting on getting hired:

"Let's see, who needs to have me run an errand?"

When no one answered, he vented his anger and began to insult them, saying:

"Prissy bunch of rich pricks—all of you suckers—who won't help a veteran of the wars! If it hadn't been for me, you ungrateful cocks, you'd be suffering with the terrible conservatives on top of you!" Sometimes he used vile words that scared away the ladies. Or he'd start bawling, snot running down his chin.

"If I can't earn a few pennies," he'd ask overwhelmed, "what in hell do you think I'll eat? Scraped wind? Grated water?"

Ñoño had another quality which was a definite disadvantage for any would-be messenger, especially during the rainy season, when lightning and sparks fell from the sky to keep Santa Bárbara, the holy patroness of the village, busy. The more it rained, the greater the opportunities were for the formation of some rainbow that would jump from the depths of the Cauca river on one side and reach the craggy slopes of the opposite side of the range of Andean mountains, framing the village in multicolored splendor. The moment that any rainbow appeared, no matter how small or transient, Ñoño would hide where no one could see him and wouldn't come out of his hiding place until after the rainbow disappeared. He'd ask with his eyes shut:

"Has that rainbow gone already?"

Once, some of the adolescents, idling about as usual, found him hidden while a glorious rainbow reigned across the sky above the village and one of them said to him, knowing what mortified him, "Come on out, Ñoño, it's safe. That rainbow moved away a long while ago."

"It surely's still there," the man answered, covering his eyes with his hands.

"Yes, it's already gone," countered the lanky fellow, nudging his cronies in anticipation. And to reinforce his argument, he asked the opinion of one of his conspirators, "Isn't it true that the rainbow's gone? Do you see any rainbows anywhere over yonder up there?"

"Nope! I see nothing but a clear sky. Nothing remained of that rainbow. It's gone for good! Evaporated! I guarantee that up there there's nothing but empty sky."

Those who saw him at close range reported that he pissed in his pants the instant he saw the beautiful colors that spread out from horizon to horizon. For that and other wicked deeds they perpetrated at the least expected moments, Ñoño never again trusted adolescents. But nobody in the village could figure out the reason Ñoño had such an unusual fear of rainbows.

Once, Dr. Uribe (claiming to be a direct descendant of the famous

General Uribe Uribe), who was deeply interested in psychiatry for very personal reasons that he was never able to remedy in spite of his vast amount of reading on the subject, approached him during one of his soberer moments as though he were beating around the bush, attempting to coax out of him the secret reason for his fearing such a beautiful natural phenomenon:

"I don't blame you a bit for fearing those rainbows, Ñoño. You must have good reasons. For my part I dread black chicken. I can't even see them in paintings. Especially if they walk under a ladder."

Ñoño laughed, made a gesture of disbelief and shook his head, closing his eyes. "I'm not afraid of chicken, black or white or any color. I'm not afraid of them," he bragged, a very self-satisfied chap.

"And why would it be?" Ñoño inquired, falling in the trap so carefully mounted by Dr. Uribe. "You afraid of chicken, Doc?"

Dr. Uribe looked around, as one who is trying to ascertain that nobody is within hearing distance. In a very confidential tone, he said, coming close to him, "Well, Ñoño, I'm assuming we're both men of the world and that I can place my trust in you."

Ñoño blinked half a dozen times and at last was able to look at the doctor eye to eye. "From this mouth," he said, sealing his lips with a finger, "not a word will come out to betray your confidence in me, Dr. Uribe."

Dr. Uribe, feeling that his subject had swallowed the bait, draped a friendly arm around Ñoño's shoulder, took a deep breath and conspiratorially said:

"Not far from Medellín, near the town of Rionegro, in a place called El Peñolcito, there are some very frightening caves where I went as a boy. Well....I'll tell you that I saw there a string of baby chicks made of pure gold, about ten of them. I was stuffing them into a bag when, suddenly, a huge black chicken about five feet tall, came at me letting out sparks through his eyes and deafening sounds, like he was about to explode. He snatched away the bag and screamed furiously, 'Since you came to steal my treasures, I swear I'll take away from you all you have when you'll least expect it.' Every time I see a black chicken—even if she's regular size—, I think she'll take it all away from me, leave me penniless and naked as a lark."

Ñoño listened to the account perplexed. He kept looking at Dr. Uribe, disbelieving what he was hearing. The physician looked at him with pleading eyes and placed a finger on his own lips. "Remember," he admonished him.

"Don't worry, Doc. I'll take the secret to my grave."

"And tell me, Ñoño, since I too know how to keep a secret, why the devil does a rainbow spook you so much?"

Ñoño was glad to blurt out without any preambles what he had never confided to anyone:

"The ghost of the rainbow might swallow me, suck me into its colors and take me to its other side castrated without balls and turned into a woman!"

"Ohhhh!" declared the fascinated physician very satisfied by his interviewing technique. "Now I do understand why you're never available to run errands during a storm."

* * *

Julito, the other fool, did carry out the errands well. With a slanted cap over his small and clouded eyes, with his thread of saliva that trickled down from his mouth now and then before he could close it on time, Julito passed the time of his life running errands, at the service of the whole town, ready to carry out whatever was needed for a mere penny. He insisted that the penny must be given to him ahead of the errand so he could buy a bunch of coconut candies or licorice at his favorite grocery store before starting to work. When they'd offer him a contract with the promise of paying later, he'd say:

"Today I don't give credit, tomorrow yes!"

If that didn't get his point across, he'd add:

"The one who gives credit went out to collect."

Armed with all the sweets he sucked on with such infantile eagerness while he worked, Julito felt happy. He shared his happiness as well as his fortune with a dog that had come out of the woods on the most unexpected day and stuck to him forever. The dog was of doubtful ancestry, a mixture of a thousand currents of canine blood, discolored and hairless, with an ear dangling over his grey, beggarly eyes, which were crossed. During cold weather, the dog limped badly on dwarf legs: too short for his bulky body. He must have suffered the outrages of an assault by savage forest beasts during his early life as a pup, because not only had he lost his whole tail from its most clinging and deeply-rooted origins, but also—at a minimum—half a butt, exhibiting during his long dog's life the barbarous scars of a savage bite which miraculously didn't finish him off since it stretched from his thighs to the middle of his back. Having such a bulky body and such short legs, the one testicle his attackers had left him bounced on the ground whenever he tried to run. Of his aperture in that place that was so prominent in his anatomy, from the very epicenter of that grotesque peeled off skin, always hung a bit of red tripe that the beasts didn't rip away and which stretched out a couple of inches every time he made any effort.

"Yuuuuk! How disgusting!" exclaimed the pampered schoolgirls making a wry face upon seeing that repulsive, wartlike peeling which, at each step the dog took, opened and left exposed the raw intestine for a second before closing up again, only to reappear with the next step taken.

"Horrid! What a revolting animal, for God's sake! What filth!" they said scandalized, closing their eyes, plugging their noses and turning their backs on him.

Because he lacked a tail, Julito began to call the dog "Notail," and by that name he called him always, even though the feisty adolescents of the village, those vagrant, loitering mud wall jumpers, nicknamed him "Noass," cruelly targeting on his defect and finishing off the dog's definition once and for all. Half the town, especially the women and the clergy, called him Notail and the other half, the males, decided to call him Noass.

From his earliest days, when he was hungry—which was very often—Noass gave out formidable howls at the least expected moment of the day or night and growled his warnings to his master at the instant he detected any of the shameless adolescents who teased Julito so much.

"Notail thinks those nasty boys are after his food," Julito explained when people asked him why his dog made such a racket.

Trying to appease his faithful dog's hunger, Julito searched all the trash cans to find him food or begged his clients to feed him after running errands for them:

"You got a little leftover for my little Notail? Nobody gave me nothing today. You'd think he's fasting. He don't even ate his daily corn bread yet, the poor starved-to-death one. He ain't fussy about what he eat, just so he can swallow it."

If he couldn't find much in the garbage cans or if his employers gave too little to his dog, Julito consoled his companion, saying:

"Something's something anyway, Notail, and nothing's worse." He never referred to his dog by the other name, the vile one, unless he was mad at him.

Everybody in the village knew that if anyone contracted with Julito for an errand, the arrangement included the provision of boarding for Noass and, as soon as Julito and his dog arrived with a message, people readied a banquet of leftovers that would have otherwise ended in the slop at the hencoop or the pigpen. Noass gradually gained weight and wound up being alarmingly disproportionate and uneven, with his body disastrously swollen, overwhelming his miniature head. Still, he continued his shrill barking. He became so bloated that, upon suddenly bumping into him, many of those who didn't know him, such as lumberman from afar who seldom came to the festive markets of the village, thought they were in the presence of a rare species of pig instead of a deserving sample of the canine family. The dog could hardly turn around, having to sit down first in order to move his tiny legs in a semicircular effort, thus rotating little by little, almost dragging himself with a truly superdog effort, until he faced the direction he was about to take and then begin to move toward his new course. The people of the village used to say that the fool and his dog competed to see who could eat more, even though Julito remained lean till the end of his days.

Day or night, Julito and Noass were inseparable. They fell asleep together at the identical moment sharing the same narrow cot. The two awoke at the cock's first crow of the day. They did all the errands together. They ate their midmorning snacks—tidbits prepared by Julito's mother—next to each other. They even attended church together.

If things went well for him in his errands business, Julito would buy bakery goods for his mid-afternoon snack in one of the shops of the village, a chocolate chip cookie for two cents and a glass of creamy milk just out of a cow for three cents: total, five errands. That was living deluxe! If he was lucky that day, somebody would give him a stub of local tobacco. Then he felt happier than a retired bureaucrat. And if the heavens opened widely and smiled at him magnanimously, he would have enough to buy his favorite dish: a hot plate of chili con carne and milk pudding with a couple of doughnuts and apple pie, finished off with a hot cup of coffee. Then, life could not be better and he'd sing, saying he would not change his life with an emperor!

Barriga llena, corazón contento (Full belly, happy heart), he'd add, munching his food.

There he'd sit down to smoke, leaning against a wall on a chair next to the bakery, slowly eating little bits of his chocolate chip cookie and taking slow sips of milk to make it last, with Noass sitting next to him, whining and licking his chops, pleadingly looking up to see if perhaps his master might toss any small crumb of the delicacy his way.

"No, Notail, this good stuff I can't give you, since it ain't for dogs.

You ain't no person, Notail, remember that. And it might indispose you with a huge indigestion," he'd tell the dog.

Those who saw Julito sitting there so at ease, enjoying his feast, would stop to talk to him:

"Hey, man, Julito, aren't you working today or what?"

"No, I'm just here for a little while resting, letting my teeth do the work for a change on one of these delicious chocolate chip cookies. I'll get back to my duties as soon as I finish if somebody puts me to work doing errands."

"Not today, but perhaps tomorrow," they'd tease him. "But remember, Julito, that a stalled mule earns no rent."

When the villagers had to choose between Ñoño and Julito, they didn't have any difficulties. The women especially didn't think about the choice for too long. They didn't trust Ñoño. Even if they had to put up with Noass's presence, they'd wind up choosing Julito. They said that Ñoño could read and might open their love letters. And since he was so foulmouthed, they stayed away from him. Since Julito was illiterate and punctual, they trusted him. The only thing that went wrong with these arrangements was that the letters arrived wrinkled because he held on to them fiercely in his hand which he then stuffed into the depths of his pocket, keeping them in his fist until the very moment of delivery.

After receiving his penny, Julito would usually leave to run the errand like lightning, followed with much effort by Noass. One day a good customer handed a love letter to Julito to deliver and began to search his pockets in vain, unable to find a single cent, finally realizing he had forgotten to bring money that morning.

"Man, Julito," he said, "I thought I had put some coins in my pocket this morning before leaving for work at the ranch, but you saw how I haven't even a penny with me. Maybe I went and lost the money."

"Well, you sure having bad luck today, very unlucky," Julito commiserated, shaking his head. "But there's no hurry. I'll just wait here, wait till you get a penny."

"But there is hurry. Can't you see I have to return to the ranch to separate a bunch of cows from the herd so they'll be ready for tomorrow's market, to fit some horseshoes, and most important, maybe a few cattlemen are already waiting for me there, interested in doing business. And if I'm not there I might lose out on the deal."

"Understood, understood, take it easy," Julito reassured the man, extending both arms, making a calming gesture. "I'm the one who's in no hurry. And I'll gladly wait for you right here. Go and do your errand first at the ranch and I'll just wait for you. Your girlfriend will be at home when you return and then I'll deliver the message."

"But man, Julito, be reasonable man. After all, I'm one of your best customers. You know very well that I won't wheedle a penny out of you, for God's sakes!"

"How you mean that?"

"Mean what? Man, Julito, hurry up. I haven't got the time to follow your drift all day."

"I mean that thing you said about whee…. How you say it? Wheedle? Is that the same as asking for credit?"

The customer scratched his head impatiently and began searching for a penny again while he corrected Julito:

"No, no, no….wheedle is the same as getting somebody to give you something without their even realizing it."

"Oh, well, then that is the same as asking for credit!"

"No, it isn't, Julito, but since you bring that up, what would be so wrong with it just this once, after doing daily errands for me for two years without ever failing to get paid for your services. Neither has she failed you. Just think of how much you've made with us."

"Today I don't give credit; tomorrow, yes!"

"Let's not waste more time. I have to go to the ranch… to tame a stubborn mule! Are you going to do me the favor or not? I promise to give you three cents tomorrow instead of one."

"The one who gives credit went out to collect."

"Damn!" protested the customer. "I'm going to try for the last time: when you deliver this letter, tell my girlfriend everything and ask her to pay you; tell her I forgot to bring money today. She'll give it to you for sure, as soon as you get there."

But when something got into Julito's head, there was no way to pry it loose. He was like an old burro. His stubbornness was incurably tied to a condition of arterial rigidity that must have afflicted his brain: there he remained standing, waiting, smiling under his tilted cap, drivel oozing down his chin.

"Well, what do you say Julito?"

"Don't worry, I won't move from here."

The customer got on his horse and went to his friend's house, knocked at her door and when she appeared to see who it was, he asked her to lend him a penny, saying he was in a terrible hurry.

"It's for that…. damn Julito, but it's too funny to tell you now. Wait till I tell you about it later, my love."

Ten minutes after he left him waiting, he returned to the park where Julito was waiting.

"Here's your pay, Julito," he said, handing him the penny and his letter. "Now go on and deliver the letter. And thanks for the lesson. I won't forget it." Why hadn't he simply delivered the letter himself was to become one of great jokes in the village.

All the villagers knew that there was no force big enough on earth nor in space, to make Julito let go of any of the messages he carried stuffed in his pocket. Some of the loafing adolescents who used to entertain themselves at the expense of their fellow men, had tried to bribe him without any results.

"We'll give you five cents if you show us what you have in your pocket, Julito," they'd entice him. "That's enough to buy a whole bagful of coconut candies. Don't be so foolish, man!"

Sometimes they threatened him. Julito, drooling and afraid, eluded them, helped by Noass who growled at the rear guard. But once he was at a safe distance, he'd turn around and yell:

"Don't think I'm a fool. The fool I left at home."

If they chased him, he could outrun them all. And, above all, he had the advantage because Noass warned him in advance with his menacing growls and would try to intercept—without much success—his persecutors, retarding at least their purposes.

But when Julito reached old age no one in the village mortified him. On the contrary; they greeted him and would ask teasingly:

"Are you going to give me a coconut candy, Julito?"

And he'd answer smiling:

"A fool I'm not."

Many in the village maintained that, in reality, Julito was so clever that he feigned being a fool; that he had saved all the silver earned through the years of postal service and was rich. But the truth was that he spent everything he earned on coconut candy, shared with Noass the sausages he purchased at the butcher shop, and stayed as poor as he was born. But to fulfill his errands, he often manifested an extraordinary subtlety that wasn't at all like what people expected of a fool. He demonstrated a basic knowledge of the human condition that was outside the reach of the majority of those presuming to be luminaries; those who came from the capital, bragging that they had graduated and were so very knowledgeable, working at jobs "with necktie on"—as they said—, which was no more than positions filled through conniving political favors, where people warmed their seats and did essentially nothing but behave arrogantly and forever showing off with big words, possessors of all kinds of licenses and degrees in extra complicated fields which gave them the right to call themselves "experts." They'd become nothing less than bosses, feeling above the laws of the land, thinking they applied only to the people who walked with holes in their pants and shoes, whom they disdainfully looked down upon.

Julito was just the other way around. He was discreet. And had style. For example, when he took one of the love letters entrusted to him, he carefully chose the propitious moment to deliver it without being seen, selecting with infallible skill the most discreet situation in which to approach the receiver, without giving rise to gossip. And if anyone asked him something about the chores he carried out for any pair of sweethearts, or anything concerning them, he'd look to one side, blinking, and say:

"I say nothing to nobody. And God knows my Notail only growls and barks."

People said Julito had a lock on his mug. With a few enormous strides, while he sucked on a piece of coconut candy, always followed by his dog at a distance, with an arm stuffed in his pocket clear up to his elbow, with rips in the seat of his pants and holes in his hemp sandals or barefoot in the summer, Julito delivered any message in less than fifteen minutes, more punctual than the sunrise of each morning. Neither the rain nor the hail of the roaring Andean storms delayed him. His mother, smoking at all hours her stubs of tobacco inside out, as was the custom of many of the villagers—"To warm my soul," she'd say—tried to persuade him not to go out during the storms:

"You're going to catch a cold, Julio, if you leave during such a downpour."

"But I got to go out and work today, Mamá. Can't you see they're waiting for me at grocery stores to run errands? Deliver food. Messages," Julito answered in dead earnest, putting on his coat.

He'd find a big umbrella and turn up his coat's collar until his neck was covered, urging his dog not to get wet:

"Don't be such a fool, Notail, or the water will get you; don't walk so slowly; get under the umbrella with me or you'll get soaking wet." Noass would take a look at him, turning his head, pricking up his one ear and remain unprotected under the storm. Regardless of how much his owner called him, the dog wouldn't move. Then Julito would bawl him out and address him by his crass name:

"Noass! Listen here, Noass! May the Devil take you, Noass! C'mon quick or I won't feed you today. Don't be afraid of the storm; it won't bite you. If you don't come right away, I'll be punish you! Don't make me lose patience. The blood is already going up to my head!"

During the courtships of most of the lovers in town Julito served them as their only messenger, without ever failing the lovers, without even once being late, giving away a bargain for a service that was without precedent in the history of Colombia. Such was the best local postal service ever known in that country and perhaps in the whole Western Hemisphere; one that couldn't be matched with any other, especially in our modern times. Not for a penny! And to those who criticized or were inconvenienced by Julito's stubbornness, it should be enough to ask of them: Where the hell can be found a post office whose bureaucratic regulations don't require payment in advance?

The force of life

Shortly after a gypsy told him his destiny was about to change, Don Alejandro, tired of using borrowed horses, found his own method of transportation: a stallion he named Bonbón. It was the most rebellious and beautiful of the herd of wild horses that a cattleman sold him in the river port of La Pintada. He tamed all of them, saving Bonbón for last. He resold the others with very handsome profits in the same town, but from the moment he laid eyes on the white stallion he didn't want to ride on any other horse.

The stallion's whiteness got confused with the fog and people were startled to see him running like a thunderbolt through the streets of the village, Bonbón's long tail and abundant mane floating in the wind and the gigantic man on top with his locks of fiery hair, his muleteer's belt bag and his white poncho flopping in the midst of the wild run. The villagers, making way for them, saluted when they flew past them, as though they were seeing an apparition that came out of the sierras and then disappeared by the narrow streets in the thick fog.

Bonbón responded to every wish of his master's hand which, without being harsh, was firm and secure, with neither the tremor of hesitations nor brusque movements, even when they walked next to the precipices that suddenly opened by the heights where they journeyed through the Andean cordillera.

The beast trusted his master because he smelled of mountain and sweat. The horse loved his master because after the long day's toil in the trails he encouraged him with a few pats on the neck, and when the man got off he slackened the cinch and brought him a little piece of sugar cane, caressing him with the murmur of his powerful voice.

"My Bonbón, my Bonbón," he called him. And the horse would get close, shoving him softly with his muzzle, looking at him straight in the eyes without having to stoop.

That is how things were between them since the day when, still as a young colt, Don Alejandro tamed him. He curbed that primitive wild ferocity without harming the animal, without breaking the spirit of the wilderness that beat in the great heart of the beast, often making his whole body tremble.

The man's neighbors made a wide circle around them each morning in the corral, to see Bonbón bucking, unable to believe that such a frisky stallion, about to take flight at any moment, would allow placing the saddle girth, the strap and the stirrups on his wild body.

No one in the village who had seen him riding up the hills on his horse would ever forget them. They were like a supernatural vision in the mountains.

During the years when Don Alejandro began to populate the province by breeding the herds of cattle he brought from Ecuador, he spent most of his days on his horse. Each time he came down the mountain toward La Pintada, headed toward the south, upriver, he stayed with his horse for a couple of days among the unexplored canyons of The Cliffs's slopes where he used to hunt and fish during his childhood. There he went to meditate each time that his spirit needed it. When he'd reappear from his seclusion, mounted on Bonbón, his strength was renewed, fresh energies bursting out of his being. Anyone who talked to him could soon sense his formidable vitality. He appeared with Bonbón in the villages of the river's basin, where they knew he was coming, with such disarming self confidence that the villagers were eager to enjoy his presence, men offering him friendship, the women love.

He lived in the Street of Heights, from where the enormous twin peaks, The Cliffs, could be seen bursting out of the valley below, and in his eyes of light blue sky which looked beyond that horizon of knotted mountains, nestled a millenary dream that not even he understood, though it burst out daily as an insatiable thirst for life. It was that thirst which led him to have twenty-two legitimate children and a stream of progeny springing sporadically by the bridle paths where he rode on his horse through day long stretches from the steep mountains of his Antioquia all the way to Ecuador, where he purchased the cattle that he raised in Santa Bárbara.

In those days the flocks of wild geese darkened the sun as they flew above the Andean peaks, followed by ducks and what they called scissortails—marine birds from distant places to the north—pursuing the mating calls that led them beyond the impenetrable jungles of Urabá. They were headed south and, while Bonbón grazed nearby, Don Alejandro used to lie upon the fresh grass by the gentle footpaths in the outskirts of the village and looking enraptured at that resplendent landscape of his country, he dreamed about the worlds that existed beyond the horizons where the birds disappeared in the midst of clouds which, like silver ships, made their rounds by the steep cordilleras.

Silence reigned in the village and the ceiba tree on the main square was still alive. Santa Bárbara had about three thousand inhabitants and it was said that it was the village built on the sharpest edge of any mountain in the continent. By a steep hillside of the lofty Central Cordillera, its stony streets converged upon the long main street that wound around the very edge of the mountain. It was only a slight exaggeration to say, as many did, that if one stood in the middle of the town and took a step to the right *or* to the left, one's neck was in imminent danger of being broken in one of the two horrendous crags that yawned dangerously on both sides of the town. The main street led to the park of the fountain in front of the church on the South, with its tower and clock of four faces that could be seen from great distances in all directions. That clock, made in Switzerland, was automatically set by a complicated system of chain pulleys and springs so the bells in the tower's belfry could peal precisely every fifteen minutes of the day and night. One chime indicated the quarter after hours as well as the three quarters; two chimes, the half hours; and the hours resonated stronger in the second beat of the toll:

"*Tin taaaaannnn! Tin taaaaannnn! Tin taaaaannnn!*

Nothing existed in the village that was more exact than the ringing of those bells. The sound of those bells was what the villagers most depended on, something that was as much a part of their lives as the fresh air they breathed. All their activities were framed by the ringing of those bells and nothing lived that gave more encouragement, more certainty, that brought greater peace, even though it be one o'clock in the morning, in the midst of a cloudy night numb with cold, when the heart felt desolate:

Tin taaaaannnnnnnn!

Don Alejandro's reputation as the winner of bouts of strength and resistance, champion of multiple horse races in the fairs with Bonbón, followed him wherever he went. His fame reached all the way to Quito.

The fairs in Santa Bárbara lasted from Wednesday mornings till Sunday afternoons, once a month. The horse races were generally programmed for Saturday noon and they were the highlight of the fair. Bonbón was established as the winner for the three years he had participated. But a young man of formidable courage who lived in one of the hills outside Santa Bárbara, was intent on beating him. Ramón Dávila went to a famed Quarter Horse racing farm of Kentucky's blue grass and found a very fine mare which he paired with a moorish horse he bought at a public auction in Medellín. The fruit of this union was the colt that Ramón called *Cervecero*—Beerguzzler—, saying that he selected the name because the animal drank beer every time it was offered to him. Once Beerguzzler developed his muscles and demonstrated he could compete, Ramón entered him in various minor horse races that took place at the town's fair, hoping to use those experiences as training for races of greater prestige at the capital's hippodrome. A few months after Beerguzzler began to compete, he became well known in the county. He easily won a few preliminary races, causing such enthusiasm among the villagers that they began to clamor for the definitive race where Bonbón and Beerguzzler would confront each other to establish once and for all which was the champion.

When the townsfolk found out that their two favorite horses would compete against each other in a race without other competitors, an unrestrained anticipation spread throughout the whole county and many said that people would come all the way from the capital of the province, Medellín, to witness the duel. The judges opted for an unusual three kilometer race in the last and most important fair of the year. The finish line was the very park of the fountain in the center of town, where all the people jammed in to make bets, the men filling up the cantinas that had proliferated around the blocks next to the plaza in front of the church, which they all called La Catedral, even though it was no bigger than the usual small town church.

Since both Ramón Dávila and Don Alejandro insisted on riding their horses, the judges had to figure out what loads to place on Beerguzzler to equal the weights carried by the two horses, Don Alejandro being so much taller and heavier than Ramón.

A few moments after the race began up the mountainside, Beerguzzler took the lead, expanding it during the first half of the race, leaving Bonbón so far behind that it seemed impossible to catch up. Regardless of how Don Alejandro tried to stimulate Bonbón, he remained far back, without the vigor he had always exhibited.

When the horses reached the outskirts of the village and began their ascent up the main street that led to the park of the fountain and the finishing line, Bonbón began to tremble. The horse sniffed the air and desperately took in large breaths, thrusting his whole body forward as though some primitive design outside human comprehension were propelling him. He moved with such speed that Don Alejandro had to grab the horn to keep from falling. Half a block away from the finish line, Beerguzzler was still ahead, but Bonbón was gaining ground on him with each step of the way, the people crushing each other on the sidewalks to open the path for them, cheering, each of them rooting for the horse they had bet on. When the horses reached the plaza, the crowd burst out in deafening shouts, feverish with enthusiasm, seeing the marvelous spectacle of those beasts disputing the championship. As they approached the finish line, Don Alejandro realized that Bonbón was running for some strange reason that had nothing to do with the race.

A few feet from the end of the race the two horses were even, but Bonbón's stride resembled the pace of a runaway horse rather than a racer's: he bolted, accelerating with such intensity that he seemed to glide, taking off with an overwhelming vehemence, scaring the people with his lightning velocity, leaving Beerguzzler behind before the astonished multitude who could not believe what they were witnessing and the astounded Ramón Dávila, who remained with his mouth open from the surprise at seeing Bonbón and Don Alejandro rush past him like possessed spirits chased by demons.

Bonbón won the trophy and the people continued yelling while they raised their arms, their ponchos flapping wildly:

"Bon-bón! Bon-bón! Bon-bón! Bon-bón!"

But Bonbón didn't stop after he left the finishing line behind. On the contrary, his step was accelerated in spite of Don Alejandro's efforts to stop him, telling him he'd won the race, ordering him to ease off. Bonbón leaped over the watering tanks and, cutting through the dispersing crowd, he headed toward the immense ceiba tree that was in the middle of the park. Don Alejandro, seeing the extended lower branches of the gigantic tree, had to choose between getting crushed against those branches or jump off the horse. At the instant when they arrived under the shadow of the ceiba, he jumped and fell tumbling upon the grass and the patches of earth.

Bonbón, feeling freer without the heavy weight of his master, gave wings to his feet and, neighing, accelerated his uncontrollable headlong run toward the other side of town. Don Alejandro, with a broken arm and his head bloodied, asked to borrow another horse to search for Bonbón.

He found Bonbón at the foot of a stone hillside, his flesh torn by a barbed wire fence that was all twisted around his body, drenched in blood, with both his back legs broken, his eyes bulging terrorized. All the way from the other side of the village he had smelled the scent of the mare in heat who was eating grass a few meters away from him. Don Alejandro got off the horse he was riding to examine Bonbón, immediately realizing what had happened and his condition. He caressed him and soothed him with that voice that always calmed him from the time he was tamed:

"My Bonbón, my Bonbón. Easy, easy boy. I know how it must feel. We're both alike, Bonbón." A vague murmur of a neigh of recognition touched the nostrils of the immobile horse stretched on the ground. "I'll be right back, Bonbón, don't worry. In a little while, nothing will hurt you anymore."

When he returned a few minutes later, he was armed with a rifle whose bullets he discharged in the back of Bonbón's wounded head. And with his good arm, he dug a ditch with the help of friends who came to see what had happened, a grave where they buried the animal. In the village they said that both the hearts of the horse and his master had burst that day, one from running, who died; and the other from sadness, who lived.

From that time on, all the horses and mares that Don Alejandro mounted looked so much like Bonbón, that years after the happenings narrated here, many superstitious people from the village began to believe that his new beasts—Hurricane, The Argentinean, Diamond and the mare Snow-white—were reincarnations of Bonbón. So much so that many of the old pious ladies, when they'd see one of the mounts appear in the hills, made the sign of the cross on themselves and said:

"There comes Bonbón's ghost. Pardon, my God, the souls of Purgatory."

The death of his favorite horse and the fact that it died for having followed the scent of the mare in heat, left a profound impression on Don Alejandro.

"It was the very force of life that killed him," he told his friends in a muted voice. "It's the greatest and most beautiful power that exists but also the most difficult to live with."

The magnificent Quarter Horse's offspring–Beerguzzler–went on to win many races at the hippodromes of the biggest cities in Latin America.